Unexpected Packages

Sindee Lynn

Passionate Writer Publishing

Indiana

Passionate Writer Publishing

www.passionatewriterpublishing.com

This book is a work of fiction. Names, characters, places, and incidents either are products of the author's imagination or are used fictitiously. Any resemblance to actual events or locales or persons, living or dead, is entirely coincidental.

©2011 Sindee Lynn

ISBN 13 978-0-9832595-3-4

Manufactured in the United States of America.

First Edition

Also by Sindee Lynn

Prince's Donor (2010)

Changing the Rules (2010)

Donor Diaries: Jenna (a PWP Short 2011)

Dedication

For all those summer nights spent chasing that elusive green motorcycle

Chapter 1

Kenny Jamison stood beside his car at his neighborhood gas station, Roger's Gas-n-More. He tapped his hand impatiently on the top of his car while he waited for the pump to begin dispensing. He glanced at the pump. Nothing was happening. Hunching his shoulders, he pushed his selection again and watched the pump this time. Still nothing.

"Aw, come on, you stupid machine, start," he said, punching the button again.

He didn't have time for this tonight. He was already late picking up Lori, his girlfriend of four months. The last thing he wanted to do was listen to her bitch about how he needed to learn the meaning of being on time.

Kenny jabbed at the start button again but got the same result. Nothing.

"Dammit," he cursed, running his hand down his face in frustration.

He glanced around to see if anyone else was having the same problem as him. Maybe it was his pump. The few people at the gas station were all looking too. Okay so switching to another pump wasn't going to help anything.

Great, he thought, hitting the button to call for help. Roger had better be able to fix this and fast.

"Yes, may I help you?"

The soft husky sound of the female voice on the other end caught him off guard.

"Uh, hi. Yeah, I swiped my card and the pump won't start."

"I'm sorry, sir, but we're having a problem processing credit card payments, and it's affecting the pay at the pump," she said hesitantly.

His eyes rolled back in his head at the obvious answer. He took a deep breath and tried to calm down. It was not her fault he had been late getting home from work and found himself pinched for time.

"Yes, I figured as much. Can you turn it on from inside?"

"Please," he added through clinched teeth.

There was a pause on the other end.

"I'm sorry. I'm not sure what you're asking me to do."

The urge to growl in frustration was almost too much to restrain but he managed. Deep breaths, he told himself. It was just the combination of leaving work late and the pressure he had been getting from Lori about his being on time that had him on edge. It was not the fault of the obviously poorly trained young person on the other end.

"I need you to reset the credit card system from inside so I can get my gas," he said slowly and succinctly as if he were speaking to a child.

Kenny realized he was probably being an ass, but at this point, he didn't really care. As long as he got his damn gas and could get to Lori's.

A longer pause came across the line.

"Hello?" He questioned impatiently.

"Yes, sir, I'm still here. I'm sorry, but I don't know how to reset anything. I can accept a cash payment on the inside."

What did she mean she didn't know how? It wasn't as if this was the first time something like this had happened. He could recall at least three other times he'd experienced this same problem with the pay at the pump. Always Roger had been able to reset something from inside the store and that was it.

"Is Roger there?"

"No, sir. But I've called him, and I'm sure he's on his way," the soft voice replied.

"Fuck," Kenny said, frustration finally getting the better of him.

"Excuse me. There is no need for that type of language."

"Huh," he said confused before noticing his fingers still on the call button.

"No, I didn't mean that to be directed at you. It's just that I'm running late, and I don't have time for this."

When no reply came, he realized she'd cut the line.

Kenny stood there with his hand on the top of his car and counted to ten. He glanced at his watch and cursed again. Maybe he should take this as an omen of some kind. Yeah, he thought, a bad omen.

He reached inside his open window for his cell phone. Dread caused a knot of anxiety to build in the pit of his stomach. There were few things in his life that truly caused him trepidation. Making this call was one of them. It was not going to be pretty. The knot in his stomach tightened as he waited for someone to answer on the other end.

"You had better not be calling me to state the obvious, Kenneth. Considering I've been waiting for an hour and a half and you still haven't shown up, I believe I get the picture that you're running late," Lori said in way of greeting.

Somehow Kenny managed to hold back the deep sigh of frustration he felt. He hated it when she called him Kenneth. It always came out sounding like an adult reprimanding a disobedient child.

"Hey, honey. I'm sorry, but I'm at the gas station, and they're having some kind of problem with the pumps."

"And you've been there for an hour and a half?" Lori asked in disbelief.

He managed to stop himself just short of putting his thoughts into words. Under the circumstances, he didn't think it would be the best approach for him to respond with the sarcastic comment on the tip of his tongue.

"No, honey, I was late getting in from work. It's been a hectic week," he said, hoping just once Lori would surprise him and be understanding.

He had tried on numerous other occasions to explain if he wanted to stay at the top of his game he had to put in the extra time.

"Apparently last week was just as challenging since you couldn't seem to be on time then either." Her remark was filled with sarcasm and barely contained anger.

Kenny ran his hand down his face. He was tired, and the only thing he really wanted to do was get his damn gas and go home. He didn't want to go through this bullshit with her tonight. As a matter of fact, he was pretty much tired of going through it with her any night. It wasn't as if he woke up this morning and decided oh what the hell he'd just be late again. Quite the opposite was true. After weeks of Lori's constant complaining about his never being on time or canceling plans last minute, he'd made a conscious decision this morning when he'd walked into his office to leave early. By noon it had turned into leaving work on time. But when five o'clock had rolled around and he had found himself still at his desk, he had realized the best he could hope for was being about thirty minutes late. Well, he guessed he'd missed that mark as well.

A deep sigh came across the line.

"When you weren't here on time and given your past history, I took the liberty of calling LaSalle's and changing our reservations for later. How soon before you get here?"

Kenny paused. A sense of foreboding washed over him.

"Well, that's hard to say. Apparently the credit card machine is down at the pumps and on the inside."

"So why can't you simply go to another gas station?" she asked in the know-it-all tone of voice that never failed to piss him off.

His jaw ached from the clenching of his teeth before he forced himself to relax. Taking a deep breath, he dove right in.

"Because I don't have enough gas to make it to another gas station," he said, preparing himself for what he knew was coming next.

And Lori didn't disappoint. He listened with half an ear as she explained all she had been through for the sake of their "relationship". And a "relationship" never worked if only one person seemed to be vested in the outcome. He could practically see her air quotation marks each time she said the word "relationship". Then she moved on to his poor time management skills, her pet peeve. Her voice increased in octave as she expounded on all the ways this could have been avoided and the many reasons why time management was so important. He leaned his head down on the top of his car in defeat and fought the urge to bang it against the shiny metal. Kenny wondered for the hundredth time why he was still with this woman. Why would he or any other reasonably sane man continue to go through this type of torture? Because she's gorgeous and looks good on your arm, his ego reminded him. Kenny shook his head. No way. He refused to believe that was the only reason he was dating Lori. There had to be something they had in common that drew him to her.

"Kenneth Jamison, are you listening to me?" Lori yelled, irritation and impatience lacing her words.

His head snapped up. Had her tone always been this annoying? It worked on his nerves like nails on a chalkboard. A frown formed between his brows to go along with the headache now pounding at his temples. He took a deep breath and made a forcible effort to smooth the wrinkles from his forehead.

"Of course, I'm listening, babe," he said, trying to keep his own frustration from being heard in his words. "You were saying how I could benefit a lot from your classes."

Whenever he was late, Lori normally rambled about that type of thing. The way Kenny figured he had a fifty-fifty chance of being right. He'd take those odds about now.

"Well, yes, I was and you absolutely can. Think of how much more you can truly get accomplished during the day if you start off with a game plan," she said.

While Lori rambled on about his poor time management and lack of concern for other people's time, Kenny wracked his brain trying to think of one thing they shared in common. He found himself coming up empty. He had always been a spur of the moment kind of person and Lori liked to plan out every part of her day. He guessed that's why she was reportedly one of the best time management experts in the city. Hell, he hadn't even known such a profession existed until he had met her.

They'd met several months back at a dinner party. One of his friends had introduced them. Kenny had found her gorgeous at first sight with her long, red hair, sparkling, green eyes and her body--well, let's just say Lori had been the total package. She was intelligent on top of it all. At the time, he had felt as if he'd hit the lottery. But that had quickly changed.

Kenny was the first to admit if it wasn't for his assistant he would probably never get anywhere on time.

But there were still times when things didn't go as expected. Lori had seemed to understand this in the beginning. It was only when they had been dating for about a month did she begin to give him "little tips". The tips had quickly turned into not so subtle suggestions by the end of the second month. They were now up to lectures lasting anywhere from twenty minutes to an hour in length. It was no wonder he'd started canceling their dates when running late instead of actually showing up. Who the hell wanted to sit and listen to their girlfriend bitch at them for an hour about being late?

Under the glaringly bright lights of the gas station, the truth of the situation smacked him square between the eyes. He shook his head in disbelief but more so in distaste. To think he would rather endure endless lectures and countless arguments on his seeming inability to be on time for anything just to have a beautiful woman on his arm. Just how shallow did that make him?

Well, that was it, Kenny thought. He knew what he had to do. He had to end things, but not tonight. He always had to build up to those types of things. He hated all the crying or yelling and screaming that seemed to accompany his ending relationships. But soon he promised himself. Having made the decision brought a smile to his face. It felt good just knowing soon this would all be a distant memory.

Beep. Beep.

He pulled his cell phone away from his ear and looked at the screen. Dammit, he'd forgotten to charge his phone at work today. Placing it back to his ear, he opened his car door and reached inside his console for his wallet. Dammit, he swore silently, when he opened his wallet to see only the black leather interior staring back at him. He had meant to stop by the bank today during a lunch he had skipped in hopes of leaving on time. The irony of the situation didn't miss his notice. Throwing his wallet back in the console, Kenny checked his pockets. Sure, he knew the odds of having any cash on him was nil to none, but he checked anyway.

"Listen, honey, can we continue this conversation when I get there?" he asked, interrupting her when his phone's low battery alert beeped again.

"Kenneth, I swear there are times when I just don't know how we have managed to remain together for this long. But I know for sure it's not due to anything you have done. I have dedicated my life to helping people manage their lives for the better by making necessary changes, and I can't even impress upon my boyfriend the importance of being on time for a date."

Kenny shook his head and rolled his eyes. Had she always been this melodramatic? He heaved a deep sigh of relief when he heard her pause. Whew! Good it was over.

"Kenny, I don't think this is going to work out between you and me."

What the hell? Wait what was she saying? Had he missed something?

"Lori, if this is about my being late tonight."

"It's not just about your being late tonight, Kenneth. You're never on time. And when you do get here, you're not really here. Your mind is always off somewhere else instead of with me."

"I've had a lot going on this month with work. I would think you of all people would understand what that means. You're as driven as I am to succeed and should know sometimes it means you have to sacrifice certain things."

Wait. What the hell was he doing? This was his way out. Lori was dumping him. He didn't have to worry about tears or buying a parting gift. It was the perfect ending to a bad situation. But as crazy as it sounded, Kenny realized his ego refused to allow him to let a woman he'd had every intention of dumping dump him first.

"I understand sacrifices. I've made plenty of them for this relationship. Do you know how badly it grates on my nerves when you're late? Or don't show up at all? Hell, you're even late for the nights we plan to have sex. I can only stay in the mood for so long Kenneth before it's gone." she said, her voice elevating a little.

An unchecked grunt left his parted lips. Who had ever heard of putting sex on the calendar? Spontaneous was how he liked to have his sex. In the heat of the moment when things just happened. How the hell was he supposed to perform to his optimal abilities under such pressure? Ten minutes for foreplay and twenty minutes for the actual act of sex. His body didn't always respond on command, and as of late, it hadn't been responding to Lori at all.

"So I think it's best if we end things now. It was fun Kenneth while it lasted. Goodbye," she said and hung up.

Kenny looked down at his cell phone to make sure his battery hadn't finally died. But no such luck. He saw it flashing in the corner of his phone's screen and mocking him. Slowly he closed his phone and tossed it in the console with his useless wallet before heading across the parking lot to the convenience store. He needed a drink. But first he needed to get gas.

Chapter 2

Opening the door to the convenience store, Kenny walked to the counter. The woman behind it had her back turned to him and was on the phone. His first thought was she had beautiful, long hair but was a little plumper than he liked his women.

"Roger, I thought you said you were on your way in. There are people who are not happy they have to pay in cash after they've already swiped their cards," she said into the receiver.

Good, she was talking to Roger. He needed to get his ass over here. His date was canceled, but he still needed gas to get home to that drink.

"I understand they won't be charged on their cards, but people have used profanity. I didn't sign up for that."

Knowing she was talking about him, Kenny felt his face heat. He hadn't meant it towards her. She hadn't given him a chance to apologize. As if feeling someone behind her, the woman glanced cautiously over her shoulder. Her eyes grew round as saucers. A rather smug smile formed on his full lips. He was used to that reaction from women. Why should this one be any different?

"Uh, Roger, I gotta go. There's someone waiting to be helped. I need you to get over here now," she said and hung up the phone.

"I'm sorry. Can I help you," she asked a little tentatively, not quite meeting his gaze.

"Hi, I swiped my card and the pump didn't start," he began, smile in place.

When she made to interrupt, he held up his hand.

"Yes, I know credit cards aren't processing. You told me already."

Her eyes narrowed and then got bigger. The frown that formed between her arched eyebrows almost caused his smile to falter before he realized it must not be for him. Someone must have come into the store, and he hadn't heard them.

"Then what can I do for you?"

The abruptness of her tone caught him off guard. Okay, so maybe the frown was for him. What had happened to the soft spoken woman who had offered to help him? Then, it hit him.

"Well, first, I'd like to apologize for my language earlier. I assure you I didn't mean it towards you. It's just I was running late for a date. I didn't have time to stop for gas on my way in from work, and now the credit cards aren't processing. It just hasn't been my day," he explained laughing softly. "And, well, I guess I just let it get the best of me for a moment."

Kenny flashed her one of his best smiles, showing off his now perfectly straight white teeth, thanks to three years of high school spent in braces. He stood there waiting for her to return his smile. After all, he had just apologized for his bad language, and he was giving her his best smile. It never failed to put women at ease and bring them around to his way of thinking. That is until now. The frown between the perfectly arched eyebrows of the woman in front of him remained. Kenny couldn't recall the last time he had gotten this reaction from a woman, if ever. At an early age, he had discovered women of all ages and nationalities found him attractive. And what wasn't to find attractive, he thought. He had worked damn hard over the years to keep up what God had blessed him with.

He stood six feet three inches in height and weighed in at two hundred and ten pounds. There wasn't an extra ounce of fat on his whole body. His personal trainer saw to it that every part of him was well-toned. From his muscular chest and arms to the six pack, he had worked hours to obtain and now spent hours in the gym to maintain. If that wasn't enough, his biracial genes had blessed him with a light brown complexion and hazel eyes women seemed to find irresistible. Well, except for the woman in front of him, it seemed.

"Apology accepted, but I still can't do anything to help you unless you want to pay in cash," she said, her face showing no signs of sympathy for his plight. "I was just on the phone with Roger, and he's on his way, but it might still be a while yet before he gets here. I'm sure you're aware that if by some chance the machine read your credit card, as long as we don't put in the request for payment, any holds will fall off in a matter of days."

Everything in her stance and attitude said she was bored with their conversation. Staring at the woman behind the counter, Kenny stood there in shock. Her expression hadn't changed with his apology or his smile. If anything, the frown had deepened the longer he stood there. Disbelief over her reaction confused him. He had never run into a woman who hadn't been affected by his looks and his smile.

Years of women constantly tripping and stumbling over their words when in his presence had given him a rather sizeable ego. And so he had begun to expect a certain reaction from the opposite sex. But the reaction of this woman was completely unexpected. Curious to discover who could resist the legendary charm of Kenny Jamison, he took his first real look at the woman standing on the other side of the counter. Cute but not his type brushed against his mind again.

She was maybe five foot eight or nine inches tall. Beautiful, long, black hair with brown streaks running through it fell past her shoulders. Large, brown eyes stared defiantly back at him, but before he could decipher what he saw, she lowered her lashes and his private link into her soul was extinguished. Curious, he thought briefly before moving past her expressive eyes onto her face. She was definitely cute with a nice, smooth, coffee complexion and no blemishes that he could see. His hazel gaze moved leisurely down her slender neck to take in the rest of her. The oversized shirt she had on couldn't hide her well-endowed chest. He loved a woman with large breasts, but typically he preferred them on a smaller frame than that of the woman in front of him. So it came as a surprise to find his body responding to their rounded lushness. It had been several weeks since he'd had sex, and his body chose this moment to remind him of that fact by throbbing to life. Kenny willed his body to stop, but by the time he'd made his way back up to her eyes, he had a raging hard on and even the disapproving glare staring back at him was not enough to quell his body's reaction.

"Was there something else you needed, sir, or did you want to go ahead and pay for your gas with cash," she asked, irritation ringing clear in her voice this time.

When she folded her arms over her ample chest, Kenny realized where his gaze had automatically fallen. His dick continued to harden painfully against his body the longer he stared at those large orbs. His mouth watered with his need to taste them. At the sound of a throat being cleared rather loudly, he forced his gaze up until he met hers. Perturbed eyes stared back at him. He shook his head in an attempt to clear it enough to think. What the hell was wrong with him? Sure, it had been a while since he'd last had sex but he must be more in need than he had initially thought to be lusting after…well, someone so far from what he normally went for. Kenny took a low breath and brought his mind back to the more pressing issue than the dick pushed against his zipper.

"I don't have any cash on me, and I don't have enough gas to get back to my house and then back again when the card processing is working. Any suggestions," he asked, a crooked grin now gracing his lips.

Maybe she wasn't into full-blown, toothy smiles he reasoned. Or maybe it was just men who stared at her chest, his conscience added. But as her look of irritation remained firmly in place, he decided she wasn't into cute, boyish grins either. Or dirty old men who stared at her chest. Okay, he screamed inside, I get the picture.

"There's an ATM machine in the back. I have other people waiting."

Kenny glanced behind him to see about six people waiting rather impatiently for their turn. He nodded his thank you and mumbled he would be back with his ATM card. Confusion followed him out of the store as he walked back to his car. Why hadn't she responded to him? His charm had been in full effect, and she hadn't batted an eye. In fact, the more he had smiled the deeper her frown had gotten. Kenny was sure there were women out there who didn't find him attractive. He had just never imagined finding one at the local gas station housed in a curvaceous, top heavy body with large, expressive eyes.

Okay, so maybe he shouldn't have been staring at her breasts. Hell, he didn't even know what had gotten into him, but he hadn't been able to take his eyes off of them. Had she even noticed her nipples hardening as his gaze had been roaming over her body? Did she know they had poked through the material of her shirt? Well, if she hadn't, he had. The thought of her getting excited by his looks had only fueled his growing desire.

Halfway back to the store after having retrieved his ATM card from the car, Kenny realized it could possibly be his ego causing him to be so concerned about the reaction or lack of reaction from one woman. He had just been dumped after all. It made perfectly good sense. He'd bet on a regular day he wouldn't have one thought or another about the gas station attendant with the large breasts. Or wonder at the mysterious look in her gaze he couldn't decipher.

Kenny continued walking towards the store, more confused now than when he'd walked out. What he needed to do was just get his cash, pay for his gas and go home. Maybe after he'd had a chance to assimilate the events of the day, he'd feel better and more himself. Yeah, he was sure of it. But as he looked up and saw her through the window, smiling at the customer in front of her, her head tilted to the side, his convictions faltered. He noticed the frown that had been between her brows when speaking to him was nowhere in sight. Something akin to jealousy crawled under his skin as he took in the relaxed way she leaned one hip against the counter. His stomach tightened at the warm smile she graced the man with. He wondered what he'd have to do to be on the receiving end of one of those.

Chapter 3

Connie Banks finished waiting on the last customer in line, a soft smile upon her face.

"Thank you and again I'm sorry about any inconvenience," she said to the man standing in front of her.

"It's no problem. You tell Roger to get it fixed, though," he responded before leaving with a wave.

She waved back. Okay, so maybe tonight wasn't going so bad. It was her first night of work, and so far everyone had been really nice about the credit card issue. Well, not everyone, she thought, gazing out the window of the store. She could see him leaning into his car. What was that a Mercedes? An Infiniti? A BMW? Something foreign and expensive she was sure. Her heart skipped a beat as he closed his car door and headed back towards the store. Dear Lord but he was gorgeous. And he knew it too. That was never a good combination.

She allowed herself the luxury of taking in every detail she might have missed while he had stood in front of her. Connie had needed to have her wits about her and couldn't afford to let down any part of her walls against the sheer magnetism of this man. But now, with some distance between them, she could look her fill.

His long legs ate up the distance between his vehicle and the store. He moved so gracefully for a man of his height and size. He had to be over six feet. And the way his shirt fit his body was a sin. It stretched across his chest, showing off his muscular build and flat stomach. And those eyes. A soft sigh escaped her parted lips as she recalled her first look at him.

He had stood there with his fingers displayed on the counter top smiling at her. Every brain cell she owned had been instantly fried. The effects on her body had been just as immediate. It had started as a simple ache, reminding her of exactly how long it had been since she'd last had sex. Her panties had gotten moist, and she had to struggle to get air into her lungs. He was in a word – hot. Then he'd opened his mouth and began speaking. The deep timber of his voice had caressed her senses leaving them aching and wanting more. It had also been what made her realize he had been the one who had cursed at her a few moments before. The knowledge had gone a long way to tone down all the effects of his overall sexiness, but just barely. When he'd been standing there giving her the once over, Connie had struggled to appear unaffected by his silent perusal. But she hadn't been able to stop her body's increasing awareness of the man staring at her. Under his intense gaze, her nipples had grown hard as if he'd touched them with those beautifully long fingers of his. It had taken everything for her to stand there with her frown in place and not shove her breasts in his hands.

The closer he got to the door Connie could swear she could see the sex appeal dripping off of him in waves. Not to mention his arrogance and bad mouth, she reminded herself. You can tell just by the way he walks he thinks it's all about him. He probably has women lined up around the corner begging for dates. Didn't he say he was running late for a date when he'd come in? She tried everything she could to recreate her shields from earlier, but her body's attraction to the gorgeous specimen opening the door was making it hard.

She looked up to see him walking through the door. Her heart slammed against her chest. Why was he smiling at her? Hadn't he gotten it through his head that neither those beautiful white teeth nor the luscious curve of his mouth affected her? Liar, her body and brain screamed in unison. Okay, girl, heads up for round two. Ding.

"The ATM machine is in the back by the magazine rack," she said when he walked up to the counter.

The last thing she needed was for him to start talking to her. Just the sight of him standing there was causing enough of a hardship on her sexually starved body.

The man paused, and she knew she had caught him off guard. She fought to contain the smug smile that threatened to lift her lips up. She could imagine he was used to women swooning and falling at his feet. Well, she was determined not to be one of those women. She would do her swooning and falling once he'd left the store and she was safe with her thoughts.

"Uh, yes, you told me that already. I wanted to apologize again for my earlier rudeness. I realize it's not your fault Roger can't seem to permanently fix the problem with the credit cards. He was having this same problem a few weeks ago," he said, leaning against the counter.

A dimmed down version of his earlier smile was in place. His gaze was level with hers. The intensity of it was trying to draw her in. *Oh, have mercy on me, Lord. Why are you testing me like this? You know I've always been weak for a pretty man. Not that they've ever been weak for me,* Connie thought. But this one was definitely giving off some pretty heavy vibes. She quickly shook the thought away. It was preposterous to think about. She'd been wrong about men in the past and she'd paid the cost.

"Yeah, well, he said he would be here in a few to fix it," she said, moving away from the counter.

She leaned casually against the low counter behind her. Perhaps some distance would make it easier for her to think clearly. She was determined not to get caught up in his eyes. It would mean her downfall for sure. When he continued to stand there with confusion on his face, she wanted to scream at him to just go get his cash and pay for his gas. Then, he could leave and she could breathe again. He stood at the counter for a few moments more before he mumbled something about going to the ATM machine. Once he was gone, Connie took a deep breath into her lungs. She was almost home free. He would get his money and leave. She wouldn't have to look into those hazel eyes of his or at that scrumptious body much longer. The bell above the door alerted her a customer had entered. She stepped back to the counter.

While Connie made idle chit chat with the man standing in front of her, she couldn't help but compare him to the man at the back of the store. He was average looking and of average height. Looking at him didn't hurt her eyes or cut off oxygen to her brain. She continued smiling at the man who was obviously flirting with her. This is more your speed, her brain reminded her. The thought didn't exactly fill her with joy.

"Thank you for your understanding. Have a good evening," she said, bidding the man farewell.

"I will. Thanks. Tell Roger I'm glad he finally came to his senses and hired some more help. And what cute help," the man said, winking at her before leaving.

Connie simply smiled. Yeah, that was her, cute. Yuck! She had been called cute most of her life. Her older sister, Brenda, was the beautiful one, and she was the cute one. Brenda was the thin one, and she was the big boned one, she thought with a twist to her lips. Brenda was the glamour model, now retired, and she was the newly hired gas station attendant. Connie shook her head as an unexpected wave of self-pity tried to claim her. She shook it off. There was no reason for it. She was working at the convenience store by her own choice, and once she was done with college, she'd be on her way.

"Excuse me. I hate to bother you, but this is not working," Mr. Gorgeous called from the back.

The man might be good looking, but if he couldn't work a simple ATM machine, then there was something wrong. It should have been enough to completely turn her off. Connie hated a man who was all looks and no brain, but when she walked to the back and saw the deep frown between his eyebrows, all she wanted to do was reach up and smooth it out.

"What's it saying?" she asked, stepping around him until she could see the screen of the ATM machine.

She was surprised to discover that next to him she actually felt small. Even though her head came to his shoulder and she was positive she weighed more than he did, his overall size and presence was larger than her body mass. She didn't think there had ever been a man who had been able to make her feel like she was, well, small.

She brought her attention back to the machine in front of her and the error message on the screen. Could it be God's way of paying him back for all that arrogance?

"The machine is out of money," she said, a small smile on her face, and headed back to the front of the store.

Her smile broadened when she heard the curse from the back. He sure did have a short fuse. That should have been a turn off as well. She hated men who resorted to profanity instead of using their brains and rational thought. But instead she found herself sympathizing with him. She sure hoped his date would be as sympathetic. At the thought of the mystery woman waiting for him, her smile disappeared. Now that was a turn off.

"Did Roger say how long he was going to be?" he asked, coming back to the front of the store.

Noting the frown between his brows had deepened, another wave of sympathy for him washed over her. Even if he was in a rush to get to another woman, no one should have the kind of luck he seemed to be having tonight. Connie didn't bother to remind herself he wasn't rushing off to another woman. He was rushing off to his woman. There was a difference.

"No, he didn't say."

"Great. It's the perfect end to the perfect day," he said, leaning on the counter with his elbows and looking up at her.

He reminded her of a lost little boy, and it melted her heart like those full blown "I am sexy hear me roar" smiles of his from earlier could not.

"Look, I don't know how much longer or even if Roger is gonna show tonight. He's been coming for the last two hours and hasn't made it yet. So how about I loan you a few bucks for gas, and you can pay me back once you get some cash."

The offer surprised even her, but she reluctantly had to admit it was because she wanted to see him smile again. Nothing could have prepared her for the brilliance of the smile he graced her with. It was ten times brighter than the one from earlier, and she could see the genuine surprise in his eyes over her offer.

"You would do that for me? A stranger? Someone you might never see again? Not that I'm like that because I will definitely be back to repay you. But I'm just curious why you would do that for someone you don't know. Or is it just to get me out of here and out of your hair?" he asked, his lopsided grin from earlier returning.

Connie couldn't help it. She just couldn't keep the joy she felt over being the cause of his returned good spirits from shining through in her own smile.

"I just hate to see anyone stranded, and you seem like a nice enough guy," she said, hunching her shoulders.

He laughed.

"That's a new one. I don't think I've ever been called *nice* before."

Mischief shined clearly in his gaze.

Not knowing how to respond, she pulled a ten dollar bill out of her pocket and rang it up for his pump.

"Ten dollars should get you where you need to be," she said, hoping to remind herself he was on his way to a date.

His being nice to her meant nothing. He was just a natural flirt. Then, why did it feel as if he were really looking at her while he was standing there? Why did it seem as if the heat of his gaze was trying to drill a hole straight to her soul? Why were her insides churning?

"Thank you. I don't even know your name," he asked, still smiling at her.

"It's Connie. Connie Banks," she said, trying to put a lid on the crazy thoughts rolling through her head.

"Hi, Connie, I'm Kenny Jamison," he said, extending his hand across the counter.

Indecision made her hesitate before taking his large hand. The moment she did, she wished she hadn't. The electricity running from his palm to hers was instantaneous. She quickly pulled her hand out of his grasp and ran it down the side of her jeans, but it didn't help. Her fingers still tingled from where they'd touched his. She glanced up at him and wondered if he'd felt it too.

"It's a pleasure to meet you, Connie Banks," he was saying as he pulled his hand back slowly. "If you tell me when you work again, I'll come back to repay you."

Think, Connie, quick, her body screamed. He's coming back. You will see him again.

"Um, it's okay, really. There's no need to pay me back."

Her insides yelled and screamed, questioning her actions. But she paid them no attention.

"Think of it as my good deed for the day. It'll get me one step closer to heaven," she continued.

His eyebrow rose in question, so she pasted a smile on her face that she hoped would add some credibility to her words. Besides, she had taken the job more for something to do than out of a need for money. As long as she remained in college and kept her grade point average up, her parents saw she had money in her bank account. Roger was a friend of her parents, so she'd naturally gone to him to see if he needed help. No, she didn't need him to come back and repay her.

"Are you sure? I mean I do have money. I just can't get to it," he said, pointing towards the back where the ATM machine sat.

"Yeah, I'm sure. Really. You'd better go. You don't want to keep your date waiting," Connie said, hoping to jog his memory he had a woman waiting for him and to remind herself of his unavailable status.

She noticed he paused in what he was about to say.

"I'm going to repay you for your kindness. I'll think of something, Connie Banks, you just wait," he said before leaving the store.

"Yeah, sure you will," she said, glancing down at the hand that had touched his.

Chapter 4

Monday afternoon found Kenny at his desk. He gazed out the large picture window behind him. There were things that required his attention. They were sprawled across his desk. But thoughts of a curvaceous woman with large brown eyes consumed him. As they had all weekend long.

He'd gone back to the gas station on Saturday evening. He had tried to convince himself it was merely to repay a debt. After all, he had always hated to be indebted to anyone. Deep down, he recognized it for what it was – curiosity. He had wanted to see if it had been his stressful day that had caused him to react so strongly to one Connie Banks. Upon entering the convenience store, he had looked around expectantly for her. Instead of her large brown eyes, he'd found himself staring into the rather dazed gaze of Tim, the regular weekend guy who covered the evening shift. Kenny had tried to tell himself it wasn't disappointment over not seeing her he was feeling, but it was just because he couldn't repay his debt. The statement had sounded like a lie then, and it still sounded like one now.

He didn't know what it was about her that had her plaguing his thoughts. He didn't need to remind himself all the many ways she was not his type. The list was endless. From her youthful appearance to her full-figured size and all things in between. But no matter how many times he'd repeatedly reminded himself, his thoughts had always come back to her expressive brown eyes, her heartwarming smile, not to mention those more than a handful breasts. Desperate to try anything to alleviate himself of the unwanted thoughts, he had called up one of his old standbys for a date on Saturday night. He'd arrogantly believed all he needed was to be distracted by a beautiful woman. Maybe even have a little spontaneous sex. But his plan hadn't worked the way he had thought it would. The whole night he had sat wondering what he'd ever found attractive about the woman sitting across from him. When they'd returned to her house after dinner, she'd invited him in for a night cap. For a moment, he had considered taking her up on her offer just to prove to himself she was what he wanted. This was the type of woman who should have control over his thoughts. But in the end, he had declined and gone home.

For the rest of the weekend he had tried everything to keep himself preoccupied from thoughts of Connie. But nothing had helped. His thoughts kept wandering back to her time and time again. How old was she? Did she have a boyfriend or a man in her life? Did she live in the neighborhood? Countless questions and no way to obtain the answers.

Pushing himself from his chair to pace his office, Kenny wasn't surprised when an image of her came to mind. Long hair flowing across her shoulders. The hardened imprint of her nipples pushed against the material of her t-shirt as she'd stood there, an irritated expression in her large brown eyes. Even the constant frown between her brows hadn't been enough to squelch his body's reaction to her on Friday night. His dick pushed against the zipper of his slacks. Or today apparently.

"Dammit," He grumbled walking back to his desk and buzzing his secretary.

Ten minutes later, he sat staring at the number on the pad in front of him, contemplating what he was about to do. Never had a woman held his interest this long without his following through, and he wondered over his hesitation. Kenny was honest enough with himself to admit if Connie were the typical woman he gravitated towards, he would have stayed as long as needed to obtain her number on Friday night. But she wasn't and therefore he hadn't. Instead he had walked out under the misguided impression he was just out of sorts. A good night's sleep would clear his head, and then things would be back to normal. A grunt left his parted lips. He saw how well that had worked.

"Okay, so what now?" He questioned aloud. "What does all of this mean?"

Hell if he knew. Never before had he found himself this confused by his reaction to a woman. There was no denying she intrigued him. He wouldn't dare insult himself by claiming otherwise. So why was he hesitating in moving forward with finding her again? Was it her size? Her choice of careers? Her age? All three? The thought brought him up short. There was no way he could possibly be that shallow. He refused to believe it. He'd never intentionally discriminated against a particular group of women. He'd just always been attracted by a woman whose career goals and lifestyles matched his. And it wasn't as if he didn't believe women of size matched that description he'd just never been attracted to one before. He paused. Women of size? Was that the politically correct wording these days?

"Okay, I have two choices here. I can either call Roger to see if I can get some information about Connie or I can sit here and continue to examine myself and find all my many flaws."

Talk about a no brainer. Forcing the nerves he suddenly felt down, he reached for the phone.

"Roger's Gas-n-More," someone answered on the other end.

"Is Roger in?"

"Speaking, how may I help you?"

"Hey, buddy, it's Kenny Jamison. How's it going?"

He'd known Roger for almost seven years, since moving to Newport Estates, the well-established and upscale community he resided in. Roger and his wife, Maureen, lived with their three children a few houses from him. He'd been over to their home for a few barbeques on those rare occasions when Roger had taken a day off. He counted him as one of his friends. He hoped that friendship would serve him well now.

"Hey, Kenny. I hope you're not calling about the credit card problems from this weekend," he said.

Kenny could imagine he'd had tons of calls about it. His heart went out to him, but being the only gas station in their prominent neighborhood came with a lot of responsibility. The larger convenience mart combos had been trying to get their foot in the door for years now, but because Roger was a part of the community, their association had always voted against bringing another one in.

"Yeah, kind of. It's really about the new girl working on Friday night," he began.

"Constance? I hope she wasn't rude or anything. She can be a bit much to take sometimes, but she's really a good kid. Her parents are friends of mine and Maureen's ya know. I still don't know why she wanted the job. Can't be because she needs the money. Her parents are more than a little well off," he said, a strained laugh sounding through the phone.

Kenny rolled his eyes in the back of his head. He'd discovered early in his friendship with Roger he had a tendency to babble when he was nervous. He couldn't imagine people had complained about Connie. He could still recall the smile she had given the man she'd been waiting on while he had been fighting with the ATM machine. His stomach had tightened in disbelief as he'd seen the man obviously flirting with her and her answering reaction to his lame line and wolfish grin. Hadn't she noticed his eyes had been glued to her chest?

"No, as a matter of fact, she did me a huge favor, and I'm trying to repay her. As you know there was the problem with the credit cards, and then the ATM machine ran out of money, and I didn't have any cash on me. Connie was kind enough to loan me ten bucks for gas, and I'm trying to get it back to her. I don't want her to think I'm the type of guy who doesn't repay his debts," he said, hoping none of the anxiousness he was feeling showed in his voice.

"Well, that sure was nice of her. Hmm, well, she only works nights over the weekend. She goes to college during the week days, studying English or journalism, if I recall correctly. She's a pretty good student, too, from what her parents say."

Kenny was barely able to stifle the groan of frustration rising at the back of his throat. There was no way he would be able to get anything accomplished being distracted like this.

"She's not coming in for anything before then?"

"Nope 'fraid not. She's scheduled for Friday night to come in at nine until three. Heck, she wasn't supposed to start until this weekend and only came in this past Friday to help me out."

Well, that explained why she hadn't been in on Saturday when he had gone to the store.

"I don't suppose you'd be able to give me her address. If she lives in the neighborhood, I could maybe drop it by her place. If she's not there, I could leave it with her parents or something. Hell, I remember what it was like when I was in school. Every little bit helps."

Was that desperation in his voice? Of course not. Kenny Jamison was not a desperate man. He could get anyone he wanted. And it just so happened what he wanted right now was the curvaceous gas station attendant from Friday night.

"Her parents moved awhile back to Arizona. Her mother had some health issues, and they said the drier climate would help. If I'm not mistaken, Constance lives with some roommates in the neighborhood now," Roger said.

So she did live in the neighborhood.

"Okay, well, maybe I could leave it with one of them then."

"I don't know, Kenny," Roger replied, uncertainty in his voice.

Kenny's jaw clenched in frustration. He was so close there was no way he could stop now. Later, he would examine the whys, but for now and his future sanity, he knew he needed to find her. To see her again.

"Aw, come on, Rog, you know me. It's not like I'm some kind of stalker or anything. I just want to give her the money she loaned me," he said, using his most persuasive voice. "You remember you asked me to take a look at your portfolio and see if you were maximizing your money? Well, I don't normally conduct business at a barbeque, but I did it because you're a friend."

"I know and I really appreciate it. Your recommendations are making sure Maureen and I will be able to send the kids to good colleges," Roger said.

"Well, now I'm asking for your help. Okay, let's forget about the address. Why not give me her number, and she can decide if she wants me to have her address."

Come on, Roger. I feel you wavering.

"Okay, I guess I can do that. Besides she is a student and might need the money," Roger said, echoing Kenny's words from earlier.

The sound of rustling papers came across the line.

"Okay, ready."

"Thanks, Roger. You know if you get those damned pumps fixed, we won't have these kinds of issues," Kenny said before saying good-bye.

Long moments passed. The number on the pad in front of him seemed to stare at him. Taunting him. He shook his head not believing the lengths he'd just gone through to get it. Oh, who was he kidding? He hadn't felt this interested in a woman in forever. And there was no use trying to convince himself otherwise. No matter what spin he put on it, there was something about the woman that intrigued him, and he wanted to find out what it was. No matter her size, her age or career choice.

Chapter 5

Connie ripped the paper out of her notebook in disgust, effectively hiding all her childish scribbling. She had been sitting at her kitchen table for over an hour and hadn't come up with one viable idea for her English paper. It wasn't like she had loads of time to complete it. It was due next week when finals began, but all she'd been able to think about was him. His chest. His smile. His eyes. No matter how often she had told herself thinking of him was useless her thoughts continued to stray in his direction. Everything about Kenny Jamison had said out of her league. From the top of his slightly curly, dark brown head to the bottom of his expensive shoes. And if that weren't enough, did she really need to remind herself he had been running late for a date? That implied loud and clear he was seeing somebody or multiple somebodies. Connie was sure a guy who looked as good as he did wouldn't be able to make due with just one woman. Now there was an extremely depressing thought. One that should have brought her back down to reality. But as Connie sat with her elbows on the kitchen table with her chin braced in her hand, she realized not even the possibility of his being taken by another woman was enough to stop her childish meanderings of Kenny Jamison. Her memories of the way he had looked at her on Friday night had only fueled her imagination. Despite attempts to convince herself the intensity of his gaze that had fallen upon her time and time again meant nothing, he had still taken up more of her thoughts since Friday than she wanted to admit. Even reminding herself repeatedly that guys like Kenny flirted without conscious effort did no good. Knowing it was probably second nature for him to caress a woman's curves with just a look didn't stop the fluttering in her stomach as she recalled how his gaze had lingered on her breasts.

Blowing out a frustrated breath, Connie got up from the table to pour herself another cup of coffee. This was getting her nowhere. The amount of time spent thinking of him made her feel ridiculous, but she couldn't seem to help it. Men like Kenny had always been her weakness, and she had the scars to prove it. Despite her age, she had been through enough heartache and tears to know there were certain kinds of guys she needed to stay away from. They were just too dangerous for her peace of mind. Not to mention her already poor excuse for self-esteem. Kenny was a living, breathing, poster child for that kind of man.

Over the years, she had learned the painful lesson of what happened when you allowed how a guy looked to affect your better judgment. When you allowed his smile to make you forget he never took you out in public. How when he touched your hand it made you forget his eyes followed every other girl around when she walked. When her hand began to shake at the unwanted memories, Connie placed her coffee cup on the counter and closed her eyes against the pain. It took a few minutes, but finally she was able to push them back behind the door where she kept them in her head. She picked her cup up once more and walked back to the table determined to put anymore thoughts of Kenny Jamison behind her. She had a paper due that was half of her final grade, and she needed to focus. Besides, she reminded herself yet again, it wasn't as if she'd ever see him again.

Ring... Ring....

A deep sigh left her as she checked the caller id. She didn't recognize the number and was tempted not to answer it. It probably wasn't for her anyway, and she really needed to get her paper done.

"Hello," she answered.

Oh, well, what was one more distraction? There was a pause on the other end of the line.

"Hello," she called again.

She definitely didn't have time for telemarketers. Then she heard a clearing of a throat.

"Sorry. Hi, may I speak to Connie."

The deep voice on the other end sounded familiar. Her eyes widened as a crazy thought raced across her mind. It couldn't be.

"Speaking."

Connie held her breath as she waited for the caller to identify himself.

"Hi. It's Kenny. Kenny Jamison, the guy from Friday night. You took pity on me and loaned me ten bucks to get gas."

Her heart stopped beating. Kenny Jamison was on her phone. How had he gotten the number? What did he want? Questions tumbled one over the other before she remembered to breathe.

"Hi. Yes, I remember you."

As if she could forget. She tried to tell herself there was probably a really good reason why he was calling. Just because she couldn't think of any didn't mean they didn't exist.

A short laugh came across the line.

"I'm not sure if that's a good thing or not."

How was she supposed to respond to that? There was no way she could divulge the truth and admit she hadn't been able to get him off her mind.

"I'll let you know when I decide," she said, cringing.

The games men and women played had never been her forte, but she relaxed a little when she heard the deep timber of his laughter.

"Ok. I guess that's fair enough."

"How did you get my number?"

She was torn between wanting to know the reason for his call and wanting to continue fantasizing about the reasons.

"I called Roger, and he was kind enough to give it to me. I hope you don't mind."

Okay. So he had called Roger to get her number. Again she told herself there had to be a perfectly logical reason why he had gone through the trouble. And there was only one way to find out.

"Why?" she asked.

"Why what?"

"Why did you call Roger for my phone number?"

Connie found herself holding her breath as she waited for his answer.

"Oh. Well I wanted to repay you the money you loaned me Friday night."

"Oh," slipped out before she could stop it. What had she been expecting him to say? That he had been thinking about her since Friday and couldn't stop. Yeah, right. Just because that's your deal, girlie, doesn't mean it's his.

"I thought we agreed it was my good deed for the day. One step closer to heaven and all."

"I never agreed to that," he said with a laugh.

"Well, if you insist on paying me back, I'll be at work on Friday night. You can bring it by then."

Connie hoped the disappointment she was feeling couldn't be heard in her voice. Had she really expected him to tell her she'd been on his mind? When would she learn that just because a cute guy is nice to you doesn't mean they want to see you again or get to know you?

"I was kind of hoping to get it to you sooner. Like maybe tonight, and as an extra thank you, maybe I could take you to dinner. I mean you really were a life saver."

Wait. What had he just said? There was no way she could have heard him correctly.

"I'm sorry what?"

"I asked if you would like to have dinner with me tonight."

"Why?"

The words left her lips before she could stop them. She had to stop speaking without thinking first. She could only imagine how it made her sound.

"Why what?" he asked, laughing.

Embarrassment had her heart pounding in her ears, and her stomach was doing flips.

"Never mind," she mumbled into the phone, playing with a lock of her hair.

Oh, God, had she really just asked why he wanted to go out with her? She didn't have a lot of experience with guys, but she was pretty sure you didn't ask why they wanted to go out with you.

"Okay," he said slowly. "So how about I pick you up tonight at seven?"

Regret over what she was about to do was already causing hot tears to pool at the back of her eyes. She was sure she would regret it later on as she ate a frozen Lean Cuisine by herself in front of the TV, but what other choice did she have?

"I'm sorry, but I can't," she said, getting ready to hang up.

She had a paper to get done and no more time to waste on foolishness. It would probably take her an hour to get her mind back on the task at hand. Great. She should have just let the answering machine pick up.

"Okay, I can understand if you already have plans for tonight. It is short notice after all. I don't know what I was thinking about. How about tomorrow night?"

Connie's jaw dropped. Was God playing a cruel joke on her or what? How much will power was she supposed to have? She had already said no once.

"Um, tomorrow wouldn't be good either," she said slowly.

She questioned her decision immediately. Her doubts only got worse as the pause on the line seemed interminable. She worried for a moment that maybe he'd hung up.

"Okay," he said, drawing out the word. "How about you tell me when would be a good time for you? I'm free all this week. You pick the night?"

All she could do was sit there, mouth open in disbelief. She tried to think of something to say but nothing came readily to mind. Then, it hit her like a ton of bricks. How could she have forgotten?

"What about your girlfriend? On Friday night, you said you were running late for a date."

He had probably forgotten he had let that piece of information slip. This proved he was no better than all the other pretty boys she had met. No matter how old, the games never changed.

"Well, we kind of broke up on Friday. Actually, she broke up with me," he said, a hint of embarrassment in his voice. "Said she was tired of me being late all the time."

Would the surprises never stop? His girlfriend had broken up with him. What was wrong with the woman? Just because he'd been a little late getting to her? She could only imagine what his girlfriend, ex-girlfriend she corrected, looked like if she blew Kenny off for something like being a little tardy.

"I'm sorry to hear that," she said, lost in her thoughts.

"Don't worry about it. It was for the best anyway. So how about that dinner?"

Every fiber of her being wanted to say yes. Kenny was the best looking man she had ever seen, and it looked like he wanted to go out with her. What were the odds? Could she trust taking it at face value? Doubts assailed her as she sat contemplating what to do next. Too many bad decisions on who to trust had soured her against believing in fantasies and fairy tales. She had given up her dreams of ever finding a Mister Right who looked like Mister Hot a long time ago.

"I'm sorry," Connie said to him as much as to her own starved ego. "But I have to know why."

"Why what?" he asked, confusion evident in his voice.

A deep sigh of frustration blew pass her lips. It was a good thing he couldn't see her face. Who in their right mind asked a guy why they wanted to go out with them? She shook her head and braced herself for whatever happened next. Well, she was sure of one thing at least; she wouldn't have to worry about him distracting her with calls after this.

"Why do you want to go out with me?"

"I have to have a reason to ask you out?"

"Unfortunately, in my experience with men, there's always a reason. Sometimes it's the right one, but rarely have I found that to be the case," she said, taking a deep breath before continuing.

"Look, I don't want you to feel obligated to do anything extra to show your appreciation for my loaning you a few bucks for gas. You've already said thank you and you're welcome. But I'm sure you have better things to do with your time. So let's just say we're even and leave it at that."

A soft laugh came across the phone line, and her spine stiffened. Was he laughing at her?

"Actually, since my relationship ended on Friday night, I find myself with tons of time on my hands. And I have never done a pity date in my life," Kenny said. "Well, maybe this once when I was in high school for a neighbor who wanted to get back at her boyfriend for cheating on her, but that was entirely different."

More laughter sounded from his end of the phone, and she relaxed somewhat.

"Is that right?" she asked, a smile coming to her face for some reason.

She liked the thought of his doing a noble deed.

"Yes, that's right. So what do you say?"

The timber of his voice had dropped. She could almost see the boyish grin from Friday night tilting those luscious lips up. She bet he was probably used to getting what he wanted and could be very persuasive when he wanted to be. As it was, she was having trouble holding onto her resolve to be tough.

"Somehow I had you pegged for a man who liked a different sort of woman. Not someone who normally picks up their dates at a gas station," she said, shaking her head.

This was pure craziness. By her calculations their conversation should have been over as soon as she had turned him down the first time. They were now on date offer number three or was it four? She had lost track. Could he really be sincere in his offer? He sure was being awful persistent.

The deep chuckle from the other end of the phone had the same effect as earlier. Her stomach fluttered with hundreds of butterflies as it washed over her, making her want to sigh from the pleasure of it.

"Okay, I'll give you that one. You are correct. I do normally date a different sort of woman, and no, I don't typically find them at the gas station. Well, not working behind the counter at the gas station," he said, laughing again.

"So why would you want to go out with someone who's outside of your norm?"

"That's kind of what I'd like to figure out."

What the hell did that mean? Connie wondered if she should feel insulted instead of merely confused.

"I'm sorry. I'm not sure I understand. What exactly is it you're trying to figure out?"

Chapter 6

Kenny suddenly found his mouth drier than the Sahara Desert. He got up from behind his desk and retrieved a bottle of water from the mini bar in his office. He couldn't remember the last time he'd been so nervous about talking to a woman. He didn't know what it was about this one that had his tongue tied and his stomach all in knots.

"Are you still there?"

The uncertainty in the voice on the other end only made the knots tighten.

"Yeah, I'm still here," he said moving to sit back behind his desk.

"Well, are you going to answer my question?"

Was he?

"Of course, I am," he replied as much to himself as to her.

But how was he going to explain to her what he didn't quite understand himself? And exactly how did you tell a woman that you wanted to know why you couldn't get her off your mind? Would she be insulted? Flattered? He hadn't planned this far ahead. Hell, he hadn't expected to still be having this conversation. Again his own arrogance and ego had made him think this would be an easy task. The simple truth was he had expected to ask her out, she'd gush or maybe become flustered, possibly stumble over her words, but in the end, she would pull it together enough to accept his offer of a date. Needless to say things hadn't gone anywhere near how he had expected them to go since she'd answered the phone. It had been he who had become tongue-tied when he'd heard her soft voice on the other end. When she had turned him down the first time, it was he who had to pull himself together and think quickly. But when she had turned him down a second time, he had become flustered and uncertain of himself. Something that had never happened before. It had been out of desperation when he had given her the choice of picking the day for their date. But that too had backfired. Now she wanted to know why. Why did he want to go out with her? Wasn't it enough that he did? Nothing about this woman was as it should be or as he was used to it being. And instead of making him want to end things now, Kenny found that it was only making him want to know more about her.

"Well are you going to answer the question today?" she asked, giving a nervous laugh.

"Sure I am. As soon as I find the best way to put it," he replied almost to himself.

He ran his hands down his face, uncertain of what to do next.

"Let me see if I can make this easier for you. I prefer honesty. I'd rather be told the truth upfront instead of being told a half-truth and end up looking like a fool later down the line."

Kenny paused in his pacing. Was she speaking from experience? He could hear a hint of hurt in her voice. He was surprised to find anger filling him at the thought of someone hurting her.

"So that being said, I'd like an honest answer to this question and all others I may ask you in the future. And in plain English please, so there's no misunderstanding about it."

He opened his mouth to respond, but no words came out. Kenny couldn't recall the last time he'd been completely honest with a woman. Perhaps when he'd been young and foolish enough to believe honesty really was the best policy. It hadn't taken him long to develop a new motto when dealing with women - tell 'em what they wanna hear. It had seemed a more realistic approach to dealing with the women in his life. But if honesty was what she wanted, then it was what he would give her. So he took a deep breath and cleared his throat.

"Connie, I asked you out because I can't seem to stop thinking about you. The fact that you are so far removed from the women I normally date has made it even tougher for me to understand why you have occupied so much of my thoughts since I met you. I figured if I spent some time with you, I could figure it out. Whatever it is," he said in a rush of words.

He felt winded as he clamped his mouth shut hoping he hadn't said too much. It hadn't been his normal smooth talk. There had been no finessing of words whatsoever. They were what they were. Now that they were out in the open, he felt exposed and vulnerable. They were both feelings he wasn't quite familiar with because he normally never put himself in a position to feel either of those emotions. Had he made a mistake in being honest? If he had fudged the truth just a little bit, would she ever have known? No, but you would have, his conscious scolded.

"Tonight at seven will be fine," she said so softly he didn't think he'd heard her correctly.

"I'm sorry what?"

"I said seven o'clock would be fine for you to pick me up for dinner. That is if the offer's still good."

There was that uncertainty again. It pulled at his heart strings. Suddenly the most important thing to him was to reassure her he hadn't changed his mind.

"Definitely."

"Okay then. Let me give you directions. I don't live far from the gas station."

He pulled out a clean sheet of paper to write down the directions. Looking over what he had written, Kenny realized she lived about three streets over from him. He wondered how their paths had never managed to cross before. Or had they and he'd just not noticed her.

"Any preferences on where you'd like to go for dinner?"

Normally he picked somewhere expensive and meant to impress. Since nothing else about Connie fit the normal, he figured he'd better get her thoughts on dinner.

"Do you normally ask your dates where they'd like to go for dinner?" she asked laughing.

At her laughter, his shoulders relaxed a little as the last remnants of tension drained out of them.

"No, not usually, but then nothing about our acquaintance thus far has been normal."

He hoped she didn't take that the wrong way, but it was the honest truth.

"Okay, I will give you that one. Where do you normally take your dates?"

Settling back in his chair, he realized though the conversation hadn't gone anything as he had planned and he practically had to twist her arm to get the date, he was enjoying himself. There was something refreshing about her. Something he hadn't seen in a woman since he'd been younger.

"I normally pick an expensive restaurant for a first date. Somewhere like LaSalle's downtown. Afterwards maybe head over to the country club for drinks in one of the private rooms. How does that sound?"

Her soft laughter on the other end of the phone brought an even larger smile to his face.

"It sounds positively … boring. I normally only endure LaSalle's when my parents are in town and the country club? Really?"

Laughter burst from Kenny before he could stop it. At least she seemed to have a sense of humor. It wasn't on his list of things he normally looked for in a woman, but maybe it should be. He enjoyed the sound of her laughter. Come to think about it, how long had it been since a woman had made him laugh?

"Do you have a better suggestion?" he asked, enjoying their easy banter.

"Nope, but I trust you will come up with a plan B by the time you get here. I'll see you at seven," she said and hung up.

For a few minutes he just sat there, the receiver in his hand. Then, he felt what could only be described as the world's goofiest grin come across his face. He checked his watch and saw it was barely pass four. Shutting down his computer, he did something he hadn't done in a very long time. He got up from his desk, grabbed his coat and keys and left work early. This was one date he didn't plan on being late for.

*****

Kenny couldn't believe it. The absolute disgust he felt was all consuming. Cursing loudly, he got out of his car and slammed the car door. He checked his watch and shook his head.

He let himself back into his house and went in search of his briefcase and the cordless phone. If he hadn't been trying to make such a good first impression or maybe this was his second impression or was it his third? Well, regardless he had wanted to do it right. And he'd come up with a plan B he hoped Connie would enjoy.

Sitting down heavily on the arm of his couch in his family room, Kenny realized he should have known things were going too well. He had managed to make it out of the office as soon as he'd gotten off the phone. When he arrived home, he had been surprised to find himself beset with nerves. It had been a while since he'd anticipated a date so much. Could it be because he'd actually had to put some effort into getting her to say yes? Nonetheless, it had felt kind of good to be excited about seeing another person.

Now as he punched in Connie's number, he found nerves of another kind taking over.

"Hello?" a female answered.

"Hi, may I speak to Connie?" he asked.

"Sure, may I tell her who's calling?"

Kenny heard the curiosity in her voice. He wondered if Connie had told her roommates about him. Well, if she hadn't before, he was sure she'd tell them now. His ears were already burning with the thought.

"Kenny."

"Hang on for a minute," she said before she went yelling through the house calling Connie's name.

A few moments later, her soft voice came across the phone lines.

"Hello."

The unmistakable excitement in her voice made his stomach ache. Dammit, he felt like a heel.

"Hi, I have some bad news," he began.

"You're not coming."

It was a statement and not a question. She almost sounded like she'd expected him to cancel.

"No, but I have a good reason. Well, maybe not a good reason. When you think about it, it's kind of lame and you would think I'd have learned my lesson but obviously not," he rambled.

"It's okay. Well, thanks for calling me," she said.

"Wait, you don't want to know why I can't make it," he asked.

Was she really going to hang up on him? This had definitely not been a part of the plan for this evening. He wondered if she would give him another chance.

"No, not really. I should have known better anyway," she said and hung up.

"Dammit!" Kenny cursed, barely resisting the urge to throw the phone across the room in his frustration.

He pushed himself off the arm of the couch and paced back and forth, the phone gripped tightly in his hand. There had to be something he could do.

Chapter 7

Almost two hours later, Connie found herself still lying across her bed staring up at the ceiling and berating herself for being such a fool. To think she had actually believed him when he told her he couldn't stop thinking about her. Well, obviously he was over it now.

Rolling over onto her stomach, she reached for her pillow and punched it into a ball. Tears burned the backs of her eyes, but she refused to allow them to fall. She hardly knew him, so what was there to cry about? Besides, she should have known better. How many times had her sister, Brenda, told her good looking guys wanted to date good looking women? Guys like Kenny dated women who looked like Brenda and her roommates. Women who cared about what they wore and always looked pulled together even when they didn't think so. When they did mix and mingle with women like her there was usually a reason. Connie's lip trembled with unreleased emotions as she recalled all the many times she'd found out those reasons too late. High school had been where she had learned just how hurtful guys could really be. After each experience, she had promised herself never again would she play the fool or allow anyone else to play her for a fool. But when you're young, there seems to be an endless supply of hope and faith in the opposite sex. So time and time again, she had allowed herself to believe the next one would be different. He would be the one to finally notice how great of a person she was in spite of her size. He would be the one to really see her for who she was regardless of what she wore.

"Yeah, they noticed alright," Connie said to her empty room.

They'd noticed her sister was on the front covers of the fashion magazines. They'd noticed she was desperate for any kind of male attention and was ripe for the picking. And, boy, had they picked the fruit! It seemed during her junior year when Brenda's career was at its height, there had never been a free Friday or Saturday night. She had loved the attention, and when her friends had attempted to tell her the guys interests were only there because they hoped to get a chance to see or meet Brenda, she hadn't wanted to believe them. But all too soon, it became obvious they weren't really into her.

Connie pushed those memories to the back of her mind where they normally resided. Since graduating high school and entering college, she had believed she was finally breaking the vicious cycle of bad luck she'd had with guys over the years. It had helped when Brenda had retired from modeling and her face no longer graced the front covers of magazines. Sure, it meant her dating life had slowed down to almost nonexistent, but it was a worthwhile trade off in her opinion. Then, he had come into the convenience store and smiled at her. She punched her pillow again and buried her face deeper into the softness. The looks Kenny had given her on Friday night had appeared to be genuine interest. But when he'd left, she'd repeatedly told herself to get over it. He was gone. Off to his woman that had been waiting for him to get gas. Then, he'd gone and done the unexpected. He'd called her to ask for a date. And then, he'd done the predictable. He'd called and canceled the date.

"I will not cry over this," she told herself as moisture pooled in the corners of her eyes.

Knock ... knock....

"Yeah," she called, her face still partially buried in the pillow.

Hadn't she made it perfectly clear she didn't want to be bothered? That was one of the downfalls to living with your best friends. They felt it gave them the right to intrude when you really just wanted to be left alone.

"Hey," her roommate, Tammy, said opening the door to peep inside.

It had been Tammy's parents who had given them the house when they'd moved to Florida for their retirement. "You got company," she said before closing the door.

"Ugh."

Who could it be? She wasn't looking for anyone to visit her, especially not since Kenny had canceled their date. Oh, no! The urge to vomit hit her as she realized who it had to be. She had called Brenda earlier to brag about her date. That was when she'd had a date. And now she didn't. Panic began to set in. She knew she shouldn't have given in to the urge to gloat. But she couldn't help it. Yes, it had been childish of her, but just once she had wanted to see the envy in Brenda's eyes as she proudly introduced Kenny as her date.

"What am I going to do," Connie questioned, running her fingers through her loose hair.

She fell back across her bed, arms spread out. She lay there a few moments more contemplating making her escape out the bedroom window. How far was the drop from the second floor to the ground below? Even a broken bone or two seemed like nothing in comparison to what she'd have to endure from Brenda. An image of her older sister came to mind. Her perfectly arched eyebrows would be raised in question and disbelief. Then a knowing smirk would appear before in her patented patronizing tone of voice she explained why these things always seemed to happen to her. A deep sigh moved through Connie as the inevitability of the situation before her loomed large. There was no way around it.

"Time to face the music," she muttered to herself.

Reluctantly she pushed herself up from the bed and walked into her bathroom. Glancing in her mirror, she grimaced. She looked like she felt. Her hair was all over her head and her eyes were shining with the tears she refused to cry over a man she'd never gotten the opportunity to know. She splashed cold water on her face and dried it with a towel before reaching for her brush to put some order to her long hair. It was her only vanity and the one thing she had over Brenda.

She'd gotten her grain of hair from her father's side of the family, who were part Indian, where Brenda had gotten their mother's more coarse hair. Her sister had fought with her hair from the day she'd been born. Her years of modeling had further damaged it. Now she chose to keep it short and freshly done every week. Connie had been born almost bald, and it had been assumed the "good hair" had passed her as well. But when she was five, her hair began to grow and had kept growing. She never had to perm it as so many of her friends had in high school, and it was always straight unless she put mousse in it to get curls.

"You can do this. Just don't say anything. Let Brenda say her peace and then walk away. You can lick your wounds later," she told her reflection.

Leaving the sanctuary of her room, Connie walked slowly down the steps. There was no need to rush knowingly into the pits of hell. Hmph, she'd prefer the pits of hell right now to facing Brenda. When she reached the bottom, she headed towards the family room but was surprised when she found it empty. Laughter coming from the living room piqued her curiosity. Why would anyone be in there? It was the only room in the house with furniture from when Tammy's parents had lived in the house.

Standing just outside the doorway of the living room, she felt as ready as she was ever going to be. She wondered if men preparing to face firing squads felt as much dread and apprehension over what was to come as she did now. Nope, not possible, she decided with a small smile on her face. Once their sentence was passed, that was it - death. No worries about a sister who would make sure you relived this night over and over again. Oh, well, it was best to get it over with. So she braced herself for the worse and moved just inside of the living room. She saw Brenda sitting on the couch beside one of her three roommates, Jamie. Tammy sat on the hearth. Connie groaned waiting for the inevitable. The moment when her presence was discovered, and she would have to explain why she wasn't on her date. She stood in agony a few seconds more before she realized no one was paying her any attention. They appeared to all be focusing on something or someone in the corner. From her spot in the doorway, she couldn't see what they were looking at. Whatever it was, it sure had their undivided attention. She wondered if she should take this opportunity to escape. But curiosity was eating her up, so she stepped further into the room and paused.

Her jaw dropped. No wonder they weren't paying any attention to her. Kenny sat in one of the overstuffed, cream-colored chairs, huge grin in place, hazel eyes sparkling with humor. Her gaze ran over him from head to toe. Her memory of him hadn't done him justice. He looked even better than she remembered. But what was he doing here. She glanced down at what she was wearing and wished for a hole to open up and swallow her. Was there enough time to get back upstairs and change before anyone noticed she was standing there? She had just turned, about to make her escape when ….

"Connie."

Busted.

Taking a deep breath, she slowly turned to face Kenny. That smile couldn't be for her could it? But if not her, then who? Connie turned to glance over her shoulder as inconspicuously as possible. Nope, no one was behind her. He was looking at her.

"I was beginning to wonder if you were too mad to even come downstairs," he said, rising smoothly and heading in her direction.

His easy swagger spoke of confidence and a bit of cockiness. He had the walk of a man who knew he would be watched by both men and women.

"I'm sorry I'm so late," he said, gathering her in his arms.

No words came to mind as she stood still as stone enjoying the feel of his strong arms holding her close. Her lids drifted shut as his scent wrapped itself around her. Oh, god, he smelled heavenly. When warm lips brushed against her cheek her world stopped. Breathe, she told her overcharged senses. Just remember to keep breathing. When he finally released her, he moved to stand beside her, one arm hung loosely around her waist. Connie chanced a glance at her friends and saw their pleased expressions, but the unasked questions shining in their eyes told her she would have some explaining to do when they had her alone.

"Kenny was telling Brenda he would probably have to do something really spectacular to make up for being late tonight," Jamie said, throwing a sideways glance in Brenda's direction.

Connie glanced at her sister, who sat on the couch glaring at Jamie. Her legs were crossed. One swung over the other back and forth. A clear sign of Brenda's agitation. She wanted to question it but found she was having difficulty focusing. Kenny was holding her hand now. His thumb rubbed slow circles on the back of her hand. A shiver moved through her body. Feeling the heat of his gaze, she looked up to find him staring intently at her. He was solely focused on her as if she were the only woman in the room.

"Ladies, if you would excuse us for a moment or two. I need to start atoning for being late."

He pulled her through the doorway of the living room across the foyer and into the family room where Connie and her friends normally received company. For a few moments, he just held her fingers captive in his. She gazed down at their joined hands, and her anxiety grew along with the silence. Why was he here? After he had called to cancel their date, she hadn't expected to ever see him again. Thoughts of his reconciling with his ex-girlfriend had haunted her all evening, and she had scolded herself for allowing him to get to her like that.

"What are you doing here?" she asked not able to take the silence any longer.

A slow grin slanted across his handsome face.

"We had a date, remember?"

"Yes, but you called to cancel. I just thought …."

Connie hunched her shoulders not wanting to put into words what she had been thinking. She lowered her gaze so he wouldn't see it reflected in her eyes, but strong fingers lifted her chin until she was forced to gaze into his once again.

"I can only imagine what you thought. But you were wrong," he said, a soft smile on his face. "Look, Connie, I know I'm over two hours late, but I was kind of hoping you would still do me the honor of going out with me."

A war broke out inside of her. Her brain was having a hard time wrapping itself around the reality of his actually being here. While the part of her that still believed in fairy tales begged for her to just accept his offer at face value. He had showed up after all.

"I don't know. It's kind of late, and I have class tomorrow morning."

It had been easier over the phone to accept his offer of a date, but now that he was standing in front of her, all of her doubts from earlier came rushing back. The fact he had admitted to being curious over why he couldn't stop thinking of her should have been enough of an indicator to leave him alone. He was only going to be around long enough to figure it out, and then he'd be gone. The feeling of misery she'd felt earlier had caught her off guard as much as it had irritated her. Tears had been hard to contain, and she'd only known of his existence for three days. What if she really got to know him only to have him leave? Connie glanced up at Kenny from beneath lowered lashes. Standing before her was a man who could easily break her heart. And that was enough of a reason for her to be wary of any kind of contact with him. No matter how brief.

"What if I promise to have you home by a decent time?"

Conflict over what she wanted to do versus what she should do caused a knot to build in her stomach. She felt her resolve crumbling at the hopeful look he was giving her.

"Look, Kenny, maybe this wasn't such a good idea after all."

She tried to remain strong in her decision to send him on his way.

"I know things didn't start out as planned. I normally don't start having a problem with being on time until at least the third or fourth date," he said, chuckling softly.

The rich tone of his laughter rolled over her bringing an answering smile to her face. But still she kept her gaze lowered until his fingers lifted her chin higher to meet the sparkling hazel eyes of the man before her. Connie blinked at the brilliance of the look in his eyes.

"Connie, I can assure you my tardiness was not due to any indecision or second thoughts regarding our date tonight."

Kenny's strong fingers refused to allow her to bow her head from his all too knowing gaze. His eyes bore into her very soul, and she knew he could see the disappointment and hurt she'd experienced from earlier as if he'd been there.

"I'm sorry if my call earlier made you think that in any way," he said softly still holding her gaze. "I'd really like to spend some time with you."

A combination of regret and longing stared back at her. It drew her in and reached out to a part of her that should have been under pad lock and key. But she found herself nodding her consent.

"Great," he said, squeezing her hands while relief shone clearly in his eyes. "Let me just say goodbye to your friends and we can leave."

Connie glanced at his tan khaki pants and polo shirt, and then at her own ensemble. After he'd called earlier, she hadn't been able to get rid of any reminder that once again she'd allowed herself to be duped fast enough. She had practically ripped the buttons off her blouse and tossed it along with her dress pants into a corner in her rush to get rid of the proof of her stupidity. In their place, she'd donned one of her many pairs of oversized sweat pants and t-shirt. They were what she called her comfort clothes. She'd even been known to go out of the house in public in them, much to Brenda's embarrassment. But glancing at his clothes again, Connie realized she wasn't going anywhere in them with Kenny Jamison.

"Umm, I need to change my clothes first. So take your time. I'll be right back."

When her attempts to move away were halted, she looked down to see her hand was still encased in his larger one. Kenny's smile grew as his gaze moved slowly over her body, taking in what she had on. Embarrassment took a back seat to the heat rushing through her veins. He pulled her back towards him until they were mere inches apart. Her breath caught in the back of her throat when he leaned towards her.

"I take it this is not what you were planning to wear for our date," he asked softly.

"No," she whispered back.

She held her breath as his hot breath fanned her cheek. His hand caressed her back and his eyes were focused on her lips. Her tongue slipped from between her dry lips to moisten them. His eyes shined brightly with barely concealed desire. If she weren't seeing it for herself, she would never have believed it. His eyes closed, and she felt him take a deep breath before his lids lifted slowly. He released her from his embrace and put a little distance between them, but kept her fingers captive in his grip.

"Don't worry about changing. I think you look fine as you are. You may want to put on some shoes though. Since I'm late, I had to scratch Plan B," he said, winking at her.

Connie's insides melted as his fingers tightened around hers. She felt her own smile lift the corners of her mouth as she followed him on shaky legs back towards the living room. Thoughts of what had almost happened whirred around in her head. He'd been about to kiss her; she just knew it and what's more she had wanted him to. Her excitement from earlier returned. All thoughts of this being only temporary were pushed to the back of her mind. She would deal with that tomorrow. For tonight, she was taking what was being offered.

All conversation stopped as they entered the living room. Connie noticed the look of disapproval furrowing Brenda's brow.

"I'll just run upstairs and get some shoes," she said, turning to Kenny.

"Constance, surely you aren't going out. You have an early class in the morning, or did you forget," Brenda said from the couch.

Connie, immediately wary, turned back to gaze at her sister. Brenda was not known for her overly caring nature especially towards her, so she knew something else must be driving the false tone of concern she heard. The question was what.

"I'll be fine for class tomorrow," she said, feeling like a child under the dark scrutiny of her sister's gaze.

"And where you're going obviously has no dress code. If you're going to any decent restaurant, I think you should run upstairs and change clothes immediately."

Her smile fell, and her face flamed with mortification. She wanted to die on the spot. Where the hell was that hole in the floor when she needed it? She heard her friends shushing Brenda. But as usual it was too late. Connie attempted to pull her hand out of Kenny's strong grip so she could escape upstairs, but he refused to release her.

"There is no dress code in affect for where we'll be dining tonight," Kenny said a frown furrowing his brow. "In fact I wish I had been able to change clothes myself. But I was already running late and my main priority was getting here. To Connie."

Connie was used to her friends defending her from Brenda's sometimes harsh statements but to hear it coming from the man beside her left her standing with her mouth slightly ajar. Never before had any of her dates stood up on her behalf to her sister. Most of them had been too busy drooling or falling all over themselves while in Brenda's presence to utter a single intelligent word. Glancing sideways, she noted the hard set of Kenny's jaw and the deep frown between his brows as he continued to gaze at Brenda.

"I'll just go get my shoes," she said softly.

Strong fingers lifted her chin to meet sparkling hazel eyes. Connie felt herself drowning in the soft look displayed on his face.

"I'm letting you go to get shoes only. I expect to see you in the same sweats and t-shirt when you come back down those stairs. Understand?"

The intensity of his words surprised her, but she nodded her understanding. This time when she attempted to pull her hand from his gentle hold, he allowed her release. She gave him a small smile before turning to walk out of the living room. She didn't get far before she turned back to him.

"Kenny?"

"Hmm," he said, pausing just as he was about to take his seat in the armchair in the corner.

"Why were you late?" she asked.

She hadn't given him the opportunity to explain earlier, but found she really wanted to know now. The sheepish expression on his face caught her off guard. The lopsided grin was back.

"I ran out of gas. I had to call Roger to bring me enough to get to the gas station."

Chapter 8

Their houses were truly only a matter of minutes from each other, and all too soon, Kenny found himself parked outside his house. Doubts over his decision to bring her here had continued during the short drive and hadn't let up yet. Despite his late arrival, there had still been time for dinner at Angelo's, a local Italian restaurant minutes from where they lived. It hadn't been his first or even his second choice, but the food was excellent and the service was fast. But when he had looked up to see her standing in the doorway, he had been both overwhelmed and confused by his need to be alone with her.

Getting out of the car, Kenny walked around the front to open the passenger door. He took the opportunity to take in a few deep breaths in an attempt to calm himself down. He couldn't remember another time when he had been this nervous. It was as if this was his first date. Ever. Thinking back, he didn't recall his stomach being tied in knots even then as it was now.

He sent a sideways glance in Connie's direction as they headed towards the front door. Her fingers were tightly intertwined in front of her. A small sense of relief came over him. It felt good not to be the only nervous one.

Kenny allowed Connie to step inside ahead of him. He didn't make it a habit of bringing women home. Even with Lori, he could count the number of times she had been here in the four months they had dated on one hand and be left with all five fingers. With the hectic pace of his work life, he wanted his home to remain a haven. A place where he could escape from it all, and thus far, he had been successful. But now as he stood back watching the woman beside him, he wondered if bringing her here would change that.

"You have a lovely home," Connie said, moving into the large foyer and looking around.

Kenny moved to stand behind her. The hint of Jasmine wafted up, and he breathed deeply of her scent. Its floral fragrance had wrapped itself around him in the car. He wanted nothing more than to bury his nose in her neck to get a better smell. Instead of following through on his thoughts, he chose to put some distance between them.

"Thank you," he said, motioning for her to follow him into the kitchen.

"Would you like something to drink?" he asked, heading for the refrigerator.

He glanced over his shoulder to where she now sat at the granite kitchen countertop. Sitting there with her chin resting in the palm of her hand, she looked so young. So innocent. What the hell was he doing? He should have taken her some place loud and full of people. Lots and lots of people. Instead he had chosen to bring her here. Was he suddenly a glutton for punishment? As soon as he had seen her tonight, his thoughts had taken a turn away from dinner to figuring out how he could get a glimpse of the real woman hiding beneath those baggy clothes. It still wasn't too late. He could say he had just needed to stop home for a change of clothes before they went out. She would never know the disturbing thoughts filling his head as he watched her.

"I'll take water if you got it. Thanks."

Pulling two from the refrigerator, Kenny carried them back to the counter. He grabbed the cordless phone. But when his gaze met hers again, he couldn't hold back his question any longer.

"Connie, how old are you?"

An amused expression passed through her eyes, and her eyebrow raised in question. He swore to himself if she said anything below twenty, he would have to take her somewhere else to eat no matter what his body said and when it was over he would take her home and that would be the end of it.

"I'm twenty-one. I turn twenty-two in two months. How old are you?"

Always he'd been proud to say he had accomplished so much in his career to be so young. But gazing into her eyes he felt…. Well, he felt old. What would someone Connie's age want in a man his age? Hopefully, the same thing a dirty old man like you wants with a woman her age, his body replied.

"I just turned thirty-four," he said, leaning against the counter.

Shock showed on her face.

"What?" he asked.

"I guess I knew you were older," she said, the look of surprise still in her gaze as it moved over him.

He could practically feel his dick and his ego swelling in unison at the appreciative look she was giving him. Damn, it was the first sign she'd given him that she found him even remotely attractive, and he was loving it.

"But I never would have guessed you to be so old."

The words were said so softly he almost missed them. At the sound of his deflating ego, he wished he had.

Interesting how her comment hadn't lessened his desire for her in the least, though.

"No, I didn't mean it like that," she said quickly, apparently noting his change in facial expressions.

"There's no good way to tell a guy he's old, Connie," he said, taking a seat at the counter on the stool beside her.

"But you're not that old."

Kenny grunted his disagreement. Here was yet another reason why he should excuse himself, go change his clothes and take her to the restaurant to eat. Afterwards, he was sure whatever crazy feeling he was having towards her would be exorcised. Hell, he was thirteen years her senior. There was no way they could possibly have anything in common.

When a warm touch landed on his hand, he glanced down to see her hand laying on his. Her fingers curled around his in a gesture he was sure was meant to comfort, but her touch was causing more havoc than comfort and she had no idea.

"What I meant is you look much younger than thirty-four. I didn't mean to offend you."

The sincerity of her words brought his gaze to hers. The genuine concern there touched him but also made him question his reaction. When the hell had he gotten so sensitive? Always before he had been proud to tell people his age. All because of the things he had accomplished to be so young. Young. Kenny shook his head. He had to laugh at the craziness of the situation. He grabbed her hands in his and smiled at her.

"Do you realize I'm thirteen years older than you?"

Connie's lids lowered, effectively hiding what she was feeling and thinking from his view. He found himself wanting to know more than before how she felt about their difference in age. Did it matter to her? Maybe she liked older men.

"Yes, I know but does it really make a difference? I mean it's only one dinner," she said, pulling her hand out of his grip and turning away.

"It's not like it'll happen again," she muttered under her breath.

He was sure the words weren't meant for him to hear, but he had and they had him thinking. Was this just a onetime thing? The question hung in the air because he didn't have an answer.

"So what do you like on your pizza?" he asked suddenly.

At her raised eyebrow, Kenny couldn't help but smile. A sparkle of amusement entered her gaze. He loved how expressive her eyes were. There was never a question about what she was thinking or feeling when he looked into them.

"It's the best I could do on such short notice," he said, hunching his shoulders in a nonchalant manner.

"This would be plan C I take it," she said with a huge smile on her face.

They both laughed.

*****

Over the next few hours, they ate and talked of everything. His job and her major in college and how they both came to their choices. He learned Connie's parents had allowed her to delay college by a year to do an internship in New York with a close friend of the family. It was during this time she realized she wanted to be a journalist. It also explained why she was not a senior but a junior in college. They discussed the changes being made in the neighborhood. Kenny had been surprised to discover her family had lived in the neighborhood for over thirty years before they had opted to relocate to Arizona for her mother's health. That had been two years ago. She talked of how torn she had been when her mother's health had demanded a change in climate and her choice to remain in school instead of moving with them. Kenny could relate to how she felt. She seemed to be close to her parents, and he knew he would have been hard pressed to choose had the decision been his to make. He was close to his family as well. Sometimes a little too close in his opinion. Even with all he had discovered, it had been her love of jazz music that had been the shocker. It was rare to find someone her age who could truly appreciate the music. They even shared some of the same musicians as favorites. When they began discussing the many jazz clubs downtown, it hadn't come as a surprise when she mentioned his favorite – Mr. Jazz Man's Place. He had laughed when she told him all the good things she'd heard and wanted to go but couldn't get in due to the club's exclusivity. Her eyes had sparkled with delight when he suggested he might be able to get her in but had left it at that. He found the fact he hadn't wanted to impress her with who he knew almost as curious as the dimming of the shine in her eyes mere moments later. He'd thought to question her about it but hadn't because he was too busy trying to figure out when he had decided he wanted to spend more time with her.

Their dinner finished, he motioned for her to follow him into the family room. Kenny resisted the urge to touch her when her body brushed against his. It was hard when all he wanted to do was pull her close to him. All evening her scent had been tempting him. Drawing him closer to her. He found himself wanting to explore all those curves he knew to be hidden beneath her over-sized clothing.

"So do you have any siblings other than your sister?"

They were now settled in the family room. He had somehow managed to put some distance between them but not enough that he couldn't feel the heat coming off of her body or the smell of her.

"Nope, Brenda is the only one," Connie answered, oblivious to the chaos she was causing.

"She's older than I am by seven years. Imagine if you can, following behind the most popular, most outgoing, most everything sibling in high school. You would think that with so many years between us the hoopla would have died down by the time I got there but no such luck."

Though she laughed, Kenny could hear the strain in her voice.

"I'm sure it couldn't have been easy," he said, fighting the urge to smooth the frown that had appeared between her brows.

"That's putting it mildly," she said, staring down at her hands in her lap. "When Brenda was sixteen, she entered a local modeling contest and won a contract with a local agency. I'm sure you've seen her before."

Well, that would explain the look of expectancy on her face when he had met her. No doubt she'd expected him to comment or fall down at her feet paying homage of some kind. Even though it was his first time meeting her, Kenny realized quickly enough he had known women like Brenda all his adult life. Hell, it was the type of woman he had been dating for the past several years.

"Hmm, I may have," he said, shrugging his shoulders.

The look of disbelief on Connie's face was laughable. He wondered exactly how long she had been walking in her sister's shadow.

"I have two younger brothers myself. With you guys being the only two, I would imagine you're pretty close to your sister despite the age difference?" he asked, studying her out of the corner of his eyes.

She threw him a sideways glance, and an odd look flashed in her eyes. He had been curious about their relationship since meeting her sister. After all, what kind of person makes a pass at her sister's date? He felt his earlier irritation return. It had caught him off guard at first, and he had thought he was simply imagining things, but when her hand had brushed against his knee for what must have been the fourth time, he had made the move to sit in the armchair by the fireplace. Even then the looks had continued, but he had paid her no attention at all opting to focus on conversation with Connie's roommates until she came downstairs.

"Why?" she asked.

Suspicion laced her words. Immediately, he knew there was definitely more to her relationship with her sister than even he had thought.

"I only ask because...." Kenny paused not sure of how he should answer.

"Kenny, I'm well aware of the fact that Brenda is beautiful. I've heard it often enough through the years, and if you would rather be with her than me, I can understand. She's not seeing anyone right now, and I can give you her number if you like. It's not like it's the first time a guy has used me to get to her."

Kenny sat there a dumbfounded look upon his face as he watched her get up and walk through the French doors out onto the deck. The look of distrust and pain that had been clearly reflected in her gaze made his heart hurt. His first instinct was to go to her and reassure her with every part of him he was not in the least bit interested in her sister, but something held him in his seat. So many reasons why he should take the out he had just been handed on a silver platter raced through his head. The differences in age, in careers, not to mention the fact she was nothing like women he normally gravitated towards. In fact, he couldn't say for sure if he had met Brenda a few weeks ago, he wouldn't have made a move. She was the type of woman he normally went for. Beautiful on the outside and shallow on the inside. Wait, where had that come from? Was that what his type really boiled down to? Thinking back over the last several women he had dated brought home the truth. A deep sigh left him as he realized he was every bit as shallow as the women he dated. Wow, that was a wakeup call. Was that how he wanted to continue to live his life? Did he want to continue to pick his women based on how they might potentially look on his arm?

"Hell, no," he said aloud, pushing himself up from the coach.

This was a new week. He didn't know when or how, but things had changed when he had walked into that gas station on Friday and seen the woman now standing on his deck behind the counter. And as much as it confused him, he hadn't been affected in the least by Brenda's good looks or the all too obvious looks of interest she had sent his way. In fact, it had irritated him, and he had been offended. Now, there was a laugh. Kenny Jamison offended by a beautiful woman sending him "come and get me" looks. Standing in the doorway, he stared at the woman who had filled his thoughts since meeting her. His gaze slid slowly from the top of her two toned head down to the flip flops she had put on her feet. He shook his head in confusion as his body responded. Yeah, things had definitely changed.

Finally giving in to the need to be close to her, Kenny walked up behind her. He placed his arms on either side of her, effectively trapping her within his embrace. A few moments passed before she leaned back against his chest. He released the breath he hadn't realized he had been holding and wrapped her in his arms. The rightness of it caught him by surprise, but he refused to fight it because whatever was going on with him and this woman was not something he could get rid of with a quick fix. Kenny realized he was treading on unfamiliar territory. Just from what he knew of her, she seemed complicated at best. But even with the doubts bombarding him, one simple fact refused to be denied, this was what he had wanted to do all evening, and he would not allow his confusion to spoil that. There would be plenty of time to think on the whys of it later when he was alone. For now, he just wanted to enjoy the feeling of finally having her in his arms.

"I'm sorry," he said, placing his chin on the top of her head.

He felt her heavy breasts rise and fall against his arms in a deep exhale before she spoke. Kenny forced his body to calm down. He didn't want to scare her.

"Sorry for what? That you asked me out or sorry you want to date my sister instead."

A small shiver ran down his spine at the thought of dating Brenda. Not on anyone's life. He wanted to reassure her that nothing could be further from the truth, but in doing so, would he reveal too much of what he was feeling? And what was he feeling? Other than lust, he thought, hoping Connie couldn't feel how being this close to her was affecting him. It was making it hard to think about anything other than how much he wanted to push her down onto one of the cushioned lawn deck chairs and make love to her. *Okay, Jamison, settle down*, he told himself. Besides, thoughts like that were not exactly helping his growing situation. Connie stirred in his arms, and Kenny realized he still hadn't responded.

"That's not what I was apologizing for."

When she turned in his arms to face him, his body moved as if with a mind of its own closer to hers, wanting to feel those soft curves against his harder ones. She lifted her eyes to his. Were those tears? His chest tightened at the thought.

"If not that, then what?" she asked softly, holding his gaze.

Looking down into her upturned face, he realized he wanted to take away the uncertainty and the pain and distrust he had spotted earlier. When in his presence, he wanted only to see her eyes shine with amusement or darken with desire. Kenny willed his dick to stop throbbing and twitching. This was not the time to be thinking of how close she was pressed against him or how her scent was threatening to rob him of his senses. Maybe if he played his cards right he might find out what it felt like to have her lying naked beneath him. He almost groaned at the instant image that flashed pass his eyes. He took a deep breath and prayed for control.

"I was apologizing for allowing you to believe I would prefer to be here with anyone but you. And I can honestly say the thought of being here with your sister never crossed my mind."

Connie gave a snort of laughter and his arms tightened around her. Never before had he met a woman so in need of reassurance of her own appeal. She was so vulnerable. He was used to dealing with women who were confident and sure in every aspect of their world. Women who didn't need him to pad their already inflated egos over their own success and beauty. But this woman ... he glanced down at her. This woman needed to hear those words, and he found it curious how badly he wanted to say them.

"Are you kidding? She's gorgeous. And you and I both know she is more your type than I am."

The glint in her eyes dared him to deny her words, and he hesitated. He wanted to reassure her, not give her more reasons to doubt his words, but he refused to lie to her. In the end it would only make his situation worse, and he knew it.

"No, I can't deny it," he replied slowly.

"And you are most definitely her type. Unfortunately."

The misery reflected in her gaze tore at his heart. All he wanted to do was make it right for her. For the pain she had felt at the hands of a sister who apparently cared nothing for her feelings to go away.

"Connie, I am here with you because this is where I want to be. I'm sure we can both agree if I wanted to be here with anyone else, then I could be. But trust me when I tell you, the thought of being here with your sister never crossed my mind."

Try as he might, he couldn't seem to keep his distaste over the thought from coming through in his words.

"Why do I get the feeling something happened tonight and you're not telling me," she questioned, gazing intently up at him.

A deep sigh moved through his body. Nothing on this earth could make him reveal her sister's hurtful words from earlier. So maybe it was time for him to change tactics. His body was definitely ready for a different kind of communication. A slow smile lifted his lips as he thought of finally tasting those luscious lips. Would they taste as sweet as he imagined?

"Can we talk about something else?" he asked, leaning close to her ear and hoping to distract her.

His warm lips nibbled on her ear lobe. He felt the small shiver running through her body and smiled into the night.

"What else is there to talk about? We talked all during dinner," she said, moving her head to the side to give him better access.

Kenny nibbled at the softness of her neck, breathing deep of the scent he would forever associate with Connie. He nipped her gently with his teeth, smiling against her neck when he heard her groan of pleasure.

"You're trying to take my attention off the conversation," she said softly.

He trailed more soft kisses up the side of her neck until he was close to her ear.

"Is it working?"

A moan was his only response. Yes. Finally he had moved them to a topic he could spend all night on. He couldn't contain a smile as he continued to nibble a path down her neck to her shoulder. His hands grew restless at her waist where he'd managed to keep them. His palms longed to be filled with the fullness of her large breasts.

"She made a pass at you, didn't she?" Connie asked, suddenly pulling away from him slightly.

He wasn't sure how much more of this his ego could take. That her mind could still be filled with thoughts other than him was starting to do major damage. Was he losing his touch? When he lifted his head, a look of triumph was clearly displayed on her face. He wasn't sure if the look was because she was the one standing on his deck wrapped in his arms or if it was because she had finally figured out some great mystery? He'd like to think it was the first, but the way his luck had been running with Connie, Kenny realized it was probably the latter.

"It doesn't matter," he said, pulling her back into his embrace.

"Like I told you earlier, I'm right where I want to be. Now I think we've talked about your sister enough for one night," he said, lowering his head once more.

"Okay, I agree but what else is there to talk about?" Connie asked in a whisper her gaze held by the intensity of his look.

"Who says we have to talk at all," he said before lowering his head to hers.

Chapter 9

Connie watched in slow motion as Kenny's lips moved closer to hers. Oh god, he's going to kiss me were her last coherent thoughts before warm lips melded with hers. Heaven couldn't have felt any better than the place she found herself when his tongue pushed its way through her parted lips and began to dance with hers. The sigh that escaped her mouth allowed him deeper access, and she gave herself over to the pleasure of his kiss.

Determined hands glided down her back to grip her butt, pulling her lower body closer to the hardening length of his erection. Heat raced through her at the contact. She couldn't breathe. Her senses were flooded with this man. His smell. His touch. Connie had been kissed plenty of times but never had she felt such an all-consuming heat take over her body as she did now. It was as if she were being sucked into an abyss. A glorious, pleasurable abyss. She wasn't prepared to handle something like this. Panic began to set in, and she pushed gently against the hard chest pressed against hers. She needed space. With him so close, she couldn't think. When his hold on her tightened instead of allowing her freedom, she shoved a little harder until she was able to finally break free. Not glancing at him, afraid of what she would see, she put some space between them.

Her thoughts were cloudy as her brain worked hard to function normally again. This was a mistake. She glanced over her shoulder to where he stood. What was she getting herself into? Connie turned away from the sight, for fear she would give in to her desire to be back in his arms again. All through the evening, she had tried to remind herself he was only in her life for a short time. Nothing would come of this. Over and over she had told herself he was used to women falling all over themselves. That she was nothing more than just a passing curiosity, and he would discover sooner than later that there was nothing special about her. But somewhere along the way, the lines had started to blur for her. A grunt left her. Who was she kidding? The whole evening had been one blurred line after the other. It had felt almost like a real date instead of a fact finding mission. The ease of the conversation while they had eaten, the things they had in common despite the age difference and that kiss …. A deep sigh left her as she recalled the way his lips had felt on hers. Her fingers moved to brush against her slightly swollen lips, but she quickly lowered them when she realized what she was doing. This was all wrong. It couldn't be what it seemed. But if that were the case, why had it felt so real? Surely he couldn't have been faking the entire evening. Especially not mere moments ago when the proof of his excitement had been pressed close against her and the desire she had seen in his eyes when she had pulled away could not be ignored. Could it? A sinking sensation filled her. She was so confused and beyond out of her element.

Connie was so deep in her thoughts she wasn't aware he had moved until she felt him behind her, not touching her but close. Heat radiated from his body to hers, and she longed to be back in his arms once again. When gentle hands on her shoulders began massaging the tension away, she gave in to her need and leaned into his warmth. A deep sigh of pleasure escaped her parted lips when he wrapped his arms around her from behind. Closing her eyes, Connie promised herself she would move in just a minute. But for now she wanted to enjoy this brief moment of being in his arms.

"Should I apologize for what just happened?"

His hot breath was next to her ear, sending shivers of pleasure up and down her spine.

"Of course not," she said quietly before turning in his arms.

The desire shining brightly in the gaze staring down at her caused her to pause. Every attempt she had made at telling herself this was not real was being trampled beneath the weight of his gaze.

"I'm just not used to all of this, and I don't know what you expect of me," she finally managed a response.

"Used to what? Being kissed?" he asked, leaning down to brush a soft kiss against her upturned lips. "Or being felt up?"

Mischief flashed briefly in his gaze before his hands moved down her back to caress her rounded backside. Moisture flooded her already damp panties, and the ache between her legs intensified. Connie closed her eyes against the pleasure his touch was invoking. Never had anyone made her feel like this before. Her body was taut with need. She realized it wouldn't take much convincing on his part to get her in his bed tonight. The thought both frightened and thrilled her at the same time.

"No, I've been kissed before and felt up. It may come as a shock to you, but I've even had sex," she said in a loud whisper as an impish grin slanted her face.

Connie didn't know where this sudden desire to flirt with danger came from. But it was overriding her good sense. The deep rumble of laughter she felt vibrating his chest caused her shirt to rub against her sensitive nipples and took the breath from her. She bit her lip to keep a groan from slipping pass.

"Do tell. Then what exactly is it that you are not used to?"

She hesitated. Did she really want to admit she may have had sex, but none of those guys had evoked any of the feelings she had experienced by just kissing him? Kenny was the type of guy who could make her forget everything life had taught her about what could and couldn't be. And it scared her more than the foreign feelings moving through her.

"Connie, we agreed to honesty," he reminded her when she remained silent.

"I know. It was my rule. One I'm now regretting," she said, her gaze focused somewhere over his shoulder.

After a few moments more of her continued silence, his arms tightened around her, and a soft kiss landed at her temple.

"Then how about I go first," he said, releasing her from his embrace.

Without having him close, the chill of the evening surrounded her, and she felt a little lost. Connie wrapped her arms around herself, hoping to recreate the warmth of his embrace, but it wasn't the same.

"If I told you how long it's been since I've actually been excited about seeing a woman for a date, you'd probably call me a liar. But the truth is the thought of seeing you tonight made me just as nervous as it excited me."

Her eyes widened in surprise.

"I mean here I was at work, my desk full of things I should be concentrating on. But all I could think about was how you smiled at me on Friday night."

Kenny looked away, but not before she saw the embarrassment in his gaze. Giddiness mixed with disbelief bubbled up inside her. To know he had been battling the same feelings both amazed and comforted her.

"Kenny, even before your first smile or your first words, I had you pegged as arrogant and cocky. A guy who was used to getting what he wanted."

"Wow, you got all that just from looking at me," he said, his smile a little strained.

"If it helps any, I also thought you were kind of cute," she said, a small smile on her face as she thought back on her first up close look at Kenny Jamison.

"Hmm, just kind of cute," he asked, an odd look on his face.

All Connie did was smile. There was no way she was gonna tell him what she'd really thought upon seeing him standing at the counter.

"The point I'm trying to make here is that you and I come from two completely different worlds. And in my experience, guys like you don't look twice at girls like me," she said, moving to lean against the rail.

She closed her eyes on the tears threatening to fall as she recalled the exceptions to that rule and all the many times she'd fallen victim to it.

"Well, they do if you come with a sister like mine."

Emotions clogged the back of her throat. She thought she had put the lid on all those old hurts and pains, but standing gazing up at the night sky, it came back to her. She'd been such a fool then. Was she headed down the same road again?

"Then how do you explain the fact that I not only looked twice at you, I practically begged you for a date and you're standing on my deck right now," Kenny asked, inching closer to her side.

Connie smiled in spite of herself. When he put it that way ... but then reality and her past experience closed ranks around her.

"I don't think something like this counts," she said quietly before adding. "You're only going to be around for a short time."

She had made herself say the words out loud in hopes of reminding herself of how true they were. When a harsh laugh came from the man standing beside her, she turned her head to glance in his direction. She noticed the muscle ticking at his jaw, which was clenched tight.

"Is that what you're counting on?"

She was confused at the underlying anger she sensed from him.

"No, it's what I expect," she said, hunching her shoulders.

Kenny placed his hands on her shoulders and turned her to face him.

"Why is that what you expect, Connie? Is the thought of having something other than just tonight such a horrible thought? Don't you want more?"

Eyes that had seen too much pain stared into his confused gaze. A soft smile played around the corners of her mouth. How could she expect him to understand?

"If only it were that simple. I'd like to think there could be more to this," she said, using her hands to encompass them both along with their surroundings. "But I've learned wanting more comes at too high of a price."

A deep sigh escaped her.

"You know I don't know any girl who doesn't have dreams of the perfect man walking into their life, and I'm no different. My guy would see no other woman but me regardless of who else was standing there. My roommates. Brenda. It wouldn't matter. It might be a day when I had on my baggiest sweatpants and biggest t-shirt. He wouldn't care how my hair looked or if I had on any makeup. He would accept me for who I am."

She glanced up at Kenny to see his reaction to her words. He was standing there with a look in his eyes she couldn't decipher.

"Would it make you happy to have this mystery guy, Connie?" he asked, moving closer.

He pinned her gently against the rail behind her. It was hard to breathe let alone think, but she didn't have to in order to answer the question.

"Yeah, it would. Just once I'd like to know what it's like to have the man every other woman wants on my arm. I've always had a weakness for pretty boys," she said, shaking her head. "Not that they've ever had a weakness for me."

A wave of self-consciousness crashed down around Connie, and she lowered her head to stare at her feet. What in the world had made her reveal so much? Would he think her pathetic that this was what she dreamed? Instantly, she knew when she had become the focus of his attention. The intensity of his gaze weighed heavy upon her, but still she refused to look up. Strong fingers lifted her chin until she was forced to look at him.

"You know I've been told by a few women that I'm somewhat of a catch," he said quietly.

Connie was barely able to contain the grunt of disbelief that rose up the back of her throat. Not forty yet and to have accomplished so much. There were limitless possibilities ahead of him. Somewhat of a catch was definitely an understatement.

"And I've heard whispers from time to time I'm what can be classified as a pretty boy. I'm not sure, but I think it's the light skin and the funny colored eyes."

Kenny hunched his shoulders nonchalantly.

Still Connie remained silent. She wondered if he had a point to all of his insightful revelations. In her opinion, he was just simply stating the painfully obvious differences between them.

Kenny ran his hands up and down her arms. Goose bumps peppered her skin where he touched. A shiver of pleasure ran through her body. When had he moved so close to her?

"So maybe, just maybe, you can stop imagining what it would be like to have that guy and start living it," he said, burying his fingers in her hair.

Connie's eyes grew wide in shock. Surely he couldn't be suggesting what she thought he was suggesting. The thought caused her heart to race unbearably in her chest.

"That was just a dream I used to have when I was younger," she began.

Kenny's brow quirked upwards, and a smile slanted across his face.

Connie couldn't keep an answering smile at bay.

"Okay, so it wasn't that long ago. But it was just a dream. Reality has set in now. Besides, there are hardly any just okay guys who don't want a girl who pays attention to her hair and her clothes. Not to mention everyone seems to want the size six jeans."

The amusement she saw within his eyes sent a chill of a different kind up her spine. Was he laughing at her? She attempted to pull away, but he pressed closer against her, effectively keeping her prisoner between the railing and his body. His head lowered until his eyes were level with hers.

"Then, I guess it's lucky for you that this somewhat successful pretty boy just so happens to like his women in oversized t-shirts and baggy sweat pants," he said before his lips brushed hers in a whisper soft kiss.

"And it's pretty damn convenient I happen to have a sudden fascination for a woman who wears size eighteen jeans."

His lips brushed hers again before she felt his tongue slip between her parted lips. Her last thoughts before giving herself over to the kiss was of how he'd known what size jeans she wore.

Connie moved her arms to circle his waist and massaged his back through the soft texture of his shirt. Heat centered between her legs at the intensity of their kiss. His hands moved between them to squeeze her breasts through her shirt. His thumbs moved over her extended peaks, and she groaned in pleasure. Her legs grew weak, and if not for his weight pressing her back against the rail, Connie was sure she would have fallen.

By the time Kenny released her lips, her heart was pounding against her chest. He had to hear and feel its incessant beat as close as he was. Connie kept her eyes closed for fear of what would be reflected in their depths.

"I think I should take you home now. If not, we'll end up in my bed. And no matter how much the sound of that turns me on, I don't think it's the right time," he said, his forehead resting against hers and his breathing coming out labored.

"Yeah," she said, snuggling closer to his heat. "I mean no. It's not."

Connie smiled softly against his chest.

Chapter 10

The ride to her house passed in silence, and that was fine with Connie. She needed time with her thoughts and time to figure out just what she was getting herself into. It had all seemed so simple while she'd been standing outside under the stars with his arms wrapped tightly around her. All her doubts and confusion had seemed groundless, but the moment he had released her, it had all come crashing down upon her. She glanced over at the man beside her from beneath her lashes. They were parked at the curb outside her house. He sat with both hands on the wheel, engine still running.

"Thank you for tonight. I had a good time," Connie said, the silence growing uncomfortable as tension settled around them.

"You're welcome. Thank you for not kicking me out of your house for being late," he replied, a half smile on his face.

More silence followed, and her doubts increased. Not more than twenty minutes ago, tension of another kind had them both thinking of nothing more than ripping the other's clothes off, but now holding a conversation was a challenge.

"Alright," she paused, unsure of what to say.

"I guess I will see or talk to you later then," she said, reaching for the door handle.

Escaping was her only thought, but Kenny's hand flashed across the seat to stop her before she could pull the handle. Connie looked down at the hand gripping her wrist. She moved her hand away from the handle and turned in the seat to face him.

"I want to see you again," he said, lifting his gaze to meet hers.

"You do?"

Joy replaced misery instantly, and a smile broke free. Connie knew it was craziness to tempt fate. At some point, this would end and more than likely with her on the opposite side of a closed door. But none of it mattered right now in this moment.

"I'd like that," she said before she could talk herself out of it.

Silence surrounded them once more as Kenny continued to hold her hand within his grip, his thumb rubbing the back of her hand as it lay in her lap.

"I think I should walk you to your door. The urge to head back to my house is just a little too strong."

He released her hand and got out of the car to walk around to her side. Connie hoped he didn't feel the trembling of her fingers as they walked hand in hand to her front door. She turned to face him when they got there.

"Thank you again for tonight, Kenny," she said, suddenly feeling shy.

"Next time I take you someplace nice."

"If you feel you have to, but I enjoyed tonight, not for what we ate or where you took me but because of who I was with," she said, staring boldly into his eyes.

The smile he graced her with was worth her bravado in revealing some of what she was feeling. Kenny closed the small gap separating them and lowered his head to hers, his eyes locked on her lips. Anticipation made her stomach flutter. Her heart rate increased the closer his lips got to hers, but a soft brush of his lips was all she received. Opening her eyes in surprise, Connie saw the desire upon the face only inches from hers.

"I have to go," he said, releasing her and stepping back.

Had Connie not seen the look for herself, she would have thought she'd done something to scare him off. But she knew he was fighting the same desire threatening to make her do something rash. Finding courage she didn't know she had, she leaned forward and brushed her lips against his, her tongue grazed his bottom lip. When he gasped his surprise at her actions, she took the opportunity to take possession of his mouth with her tongue. She wasn't as experienced as he was and her technique may have been lacking, but the groan of pleasure she heard from him proved she was doing something right. Kenny's fist tightened in her hair to hold her head in place for their kiss. When they broke apart, they were both breathing heavy. Kenny took the keys from her slack fingers and opened the door for her. He then pushed her over the threshold.

"Go to bed," he said, his voice coming out huskier than normal.

She glanced down and saw the definite outline of an erection straining against his slacks and smiled. She had done that.

"I'll call you tomorrow," he said before turning and heading back to his car.

Connie closed the door behind her and leaned against it, a huge grin on her face.

"Do you have any idea what time it is?"

Her keys fell to the floor as her hand flew to her chest.

"Dammit, Brenda, what are you trying to do? Give me a heart attack," she asked, bending to retrieve her keys.

What the hell was she still doing here? It was.... She glanced at her watch. Man, she hadn't realized it was so late. It was after two in the morning. She was gonna be tired later today for class, she thought, smiling to herself.

"Where have you been, Constance?" Brenda asked, a deep scowl on her face and a look of disapproval shining in her eyes. "If Mom and Dad knew this was how you were spending their good, hard earned money, they'd flip."

Connie simply rolled her eyes. She was in no mood for a big sister chitchat.

"What are you still doing here?" she asked instead of answering Brenda's question.

"I've been waiting for you to get home," Brenda said, standing there with her hands on her slender hips.

"As you can see I'm fine. I'm a big girl, Bren. I don't need you waiting up for me."

Her sister's hard gaze raked over her body.

"That goes without saying."

Connie chose to ignore the obvious dig about her size. It was an old hurt she'd long ago come to grips with. But still she couldn't keep the feeling of self-consciousness from washing over her at Brenda's continued perusal. Funny how the whole time she'd been with Kenny, she hadn't felt bad about being in her sweats. But two minutes in the presence of her sister, she was wondering how he'd managed to touch her let alone have a hard on for her. But he had, she quickly reminded herself. *He wanted you. You felt how hard he was for you. You saw it.*

"Brenda, I'm tired and ready for bed, so if you don't want anything, lock the door on your way out," she said, heading upstairs to her room.

"He's out of your league, you know," Brenda called after her.

A heavy sigh moved through her as she paused on the stairs. Apparently it was burst Connie's bubble time. She should have realized it was coming but hadn't been expecting it so soon. It had only been one date.

"Did you sleep with him, Connie? I mean I'm sure he pulled some moves you're not used to. Just don't hold your breath waiting for him to call."

Her spine stiffened. No matter how many times she found herself on the receiving end of Brenda's wrath, it never failed to catch her slightly off guard. And really she didn't know why because for more years than she cared to recall, this had been their relationship. Had there ever been a time when she had actually enjoyed having an older sister?

"I didn't sleep with him, not that it's any of your business," she finally answered, her back still turned on Brenda.

Connie was glad her voice came out sounding calmer than she was feeling. A part of her was yelling for her to fight back. While the rest of her just wanted to run away and hide from the cruel words like she'd done most of her life.

"Look, Con, why don't you save yourself some time and a lot of hurt feelings. Just end this farce now before it goes too far."

For the first time in a long time, Connie felt the prick of tears burn the backs of her eyes at Brenda's words. She had learned at a young age it did no good to cry over the things Brenda said because she would find herself crying whenever in her presence. So she had learned to hide her emotions, and she was determined not to give her sister the benefit of seeing how much her words had upset her now. The peace and solitude of her room was waiting for her. All she needed to do was just go upstairs and leave Brenda standing there. She continued her ascent up the stairs before pausing. The rational side of her brain questioned her actions, but the part of her that wanted vengeance for all those years of hurt feelings egged her on. After all, she knew what this was about, and it had nothing to do with her welfare.

"What's wrong, Brenda? You got your panties all in a bunch because Kenny didn't pay enough attention to you?"

A look of shock passed through her sister's eyes. Yes, Connie wanted to scream. It seems she had hit the nail on the head. Her always calm and collected sister looked a little unnerved by the comment. Her ever steady gaze had dropped a few centimeters. Connie walked back down the stairs until she was standing directly in front of her.

"That is what this is all about, right?"

"I don't know what you're talking about, Constance. This is about my not wanting to see you get hurt by a man who only has one thing on his mind. And that's how he can use you to get me to notice him or have you forgotten that's how it normally works," Brenda said, a small smile coming to her face.

It was a low blow. Normally they sparred back and forth before she went in for the kill but not tonight apparently.

"That was a long time ago, Brenda. I've grown up since then," Connie said, fighting the memories threatening to overtake her.

She was not that same naïve girl she had once been. High school was behind her.

"Oh, Connie, you'll never be grown enough to handle men like Kenny Jamison," Brenda said, her tone condescending. "He's way out of your league, honey. Why don't you leave the real men to women who can handle them?"

The implication was clear in the smug grin on her face. Every part of Connie wanted to yell and scream and tell her she was wrong. But more so she wanted to wipe the patronizing smile right off her face. But tonight was not the time. She was just too uncertain of what she was doing to get into it any further.

"Go home, Brenda," she said, brushing pass her towards the door.

She was done discussing this.

"Con, you know I love you, honey. You're my baby sister. I don't want to see another man take advantage of you and your naïveté, especially not a man like Kenny Jamison. It would just be too unfair, and I don't want you to get your little heart broken," Brenda said, stepping closer and embracing Connie.

"Again."

When Connie failed to return the hug, Brenda stepped back an irritated look on her face.

"Good night, Brenda," she said, opening the door for her.

"Fine. Don't listen. But don't come crawling to me when he tears your heart out for fun," Brenda said, flouncing through the door.

Connie closed the door and leaned against it for a moment. Fighting with Brenda was always emotionally draining. She closed her eyes, and an image of Kenny came instantly to mind, bringing a smile with it. His eyes dancing with amusement and then filled with desire as he'd turned away when leaving. The way his lips had felt against hers. Thoughts of her evening spent in his company came racing back, causing her body and face to flush with heat. Brenda was right about one thing, she thought, pushing away from the door and heading upstairs to her room. It took a certain type of woman to handle a man like Kenny Jamison. The question was could she be that woman?

Chapter 11

Kenny entered his home on Tuesday evening through his garage, tossing his keys and briefcase on the counter. He breathed his first real breath of the day. From the moment he had stepped into his office, he had been going non-stop. There hadn't been a free moment to even stop and eat, let alone....

"Oh, no," he groaned, recalling his promise from last night.

He glanced at the clock over the stove. It was after nine o'clock. Dammit, he was not making a very good impression, if he said so himself.

Loosening his tie, he grabbed a beer from the refrigerator and headed upstairs. He sat his beer on the nightstand before hanging up his suit jacket. Grabbing the phone in one hand and unbuttoning his dress shirt with his other, he dialed Connie's number. If last night revealed one thing with the utmost clarity, it was the fact some idiot or possibly several idiots had done a number on her self-confidence.

"Hello?"

"Hi, may I speak with Connie?" Kenny said, sitting down on the edge of his bed to remove his shoes.

He rolled his neck back on his shoulders and felt the tension tightening at the back of his neck. It had been one helluva day. And it was taking a toll on his body now that it was over.

"Sure, hang on," the female said.

A deep sigh escaped him as he waited for Connie to pick up. He was feeling restless, and he knew it was from the day he'd had at work. He had managed to get in early this morning, thinking to get ahead of his always hectic day and recalling how he had left early yesterday. But as he had flipped through the slips of paper his secretary had been kind enough to leave on his desk, which held his messages from the day before, he had felt the beginnings of a head ache. He'd been going since six this morning, not even stopping for lunch. There were days when he lived for the fast paced life, but there were days like today when he had wished for half a moment to pause and just breathe. Or have time to make a simple phone call.

He rubbed the back of his neck with his hand and felt the knot the muscles there had worked themselves into during the course of his day. If he didn't find a way to relieve the tension, he would never get to sleep tonight. There was another full day in store tomorrow, so not sleeping was not an option. There were few things that had the ability to loosen him up from a day like today. A few hours of hot and heavy sex was the quickest way to do the trick. Not to mention his favorite. A vision of Connie's desire filled eyes flashed across his mind, causing his body to tighten in other areas. No, it was too soon to broach the subject of sex, no matter how his body demanded he change his mind. And he refused to use her luscious body for the sole purpose of unwinding. No, the only other option was to get out. A thought came to him as he put his shoes in his closet.

"Hello."

Kenny felt a smile come to his face at Connie's soft spoken greeting.

"Hey."

"Hi yourself," came the almost shy reply.

"I'm sorry I didn't get a chance to call you today, but things were a little hectic," he said in way of explanation.

There was a pause on the line. Kenny stopped what he was doing.

"It's okay. I figured it was something like that," she said slowly.

"You did, huh? I'm not sure I believe that, but I'll let it go. So what are you doing?"

"Ugh, I'm studying for finals."

He smiled as he heard the frustration in her voice. She sounded as if she could use a break. And he wanted to see her again.

"Would you be interested in a break?"

A smaller pause came this time.

"What kind of break did you have in mind?"

"I'm feeling a little restless and thought I'd go for a ride," he said, pulling a t-shirt and jeans out of his closet.

"Well I guess I could use a little break. I have been going at it since I got home from class."

A smile lifted his lips as he tossed his clothes on the bed.

"Okay I'll be there in about fifteen minutes," he said, enjoying the excitement he felt over the thought of seeing her again.

"Okay."

"Oh, yeah, bring a jacket with you," he said before hanging up.

Kenny quickly changed his clothes before he headed back downstairs with his unopened beer in his hands. He grabbed his leather jacket out of the hall closet before putting the beer back in the refrigerator. Grabbing his keys from the hook by the door, he set the alarm before exiting his kitchen to his garage. His eyes brightened as he removed the cover from his baby. Kenny ran his hand along the smooth, shiny black and gray exterior of her body. This had been the best purchase of his adult life. Excitement and nervousness warred within him as he thought of sharing this part of his life with Connie. He wondered how she would react. None of the past women he'd dated had wanted any parts of this side of him. And it had suited him just fine. He'd always enjoyed his own company without the endless prattle of a woman, but he found he wanted very much to share this part of himself with her. As he put his key in the ignition and heard the engine purr to life, he wondered if Connie would be different.

*****

Excitement, anticipation and nerves all jumbled up inside Connie's stomach at the thought of seeing Kenny again. Not thirty minutes ago, she was cursing the ground he walked on and herself for once again allowing a guy to get her upset.

She'd been checking her cell phone for half the day before she realized he didn't have the number. After her last class, she had rushed home, barely allowing her books to drop to the table before she'd run in search of a phone. Her heart had picked up its pace seeing the red light flashing indicating messages. When there had been none for her, a dark cloud had appeared over her head. For the next three hours as she had tried to concentrate on her studies, her gaze continuously fell on the phone. Maybe he was busy at work and just didn't have the time, she'd thought optimistically. Or maybe he'd just given her a line of crock and bull crap. Her spirits had dropped a few more notches. By six o'clock with no call, Connie had pretty much reached the conclusion she'd been had. Last night had been her once in a lifetime shot. Going over the events of the previous night in her head, there were so many things she regretted. Could she have been less sophisticated? Everything about their short time together had proven to her beyond a shadow of a doubt if not to him that they most certainly did not belong together. It could have been any one of a thousand things that had turned him off.

So she had spent the next two hours or so pretending she wasn't hurting over being fooled once again by a guy she should have known was too good to be true. It was then her sister's words had come back to haunt her. He was out of her league. She had known it going into the date, but she'd still gone. She had no one to blame but herself. When Tammy had called her for the phone, the first tears had just begun to fall. It had taken her a few moments to pull herself together. But that was then and this is now, Connie thought as she glanced at herself in the downstairs mirror again to make sure she looked okay. The first date they'd had he'd seen her at her worst, but tonight would be different.

After getting off the phone with him, she had taken a quick shower and then began the process of deciding what to wear. What did one wear on a ride out? Her friends had gone out to dinner, so she'd been left to make the decision on her own. Considering they might end up somewhere nice for drinks, she had chosen a pair of simple black slacks with a medium heel. Her choice of blouses had been easier. She'd chosen an emerald silk button up she'd gotten for Christmas from her mom. It complemented her complexion and the deep v-neck showed off her assets. After having made those choices, she'd applied a light make-up and brushed her hair until it hung perfectly across her shoulders.

Hearing a loud noise outside, she pulled back the sheer curtains to see a figure dressed in black getting off of a motorcycle in front of her house. She wondered if he was here for one of her roommates or just had the wrong house.

She tried to think if any of them had mentioned seeing a guy who rode a bike. She'd have remembered if they had. She looked again and noticed the confident swagger and the way he filled out the leather jacket he had on. Damn, he had the sexiest walk of anyone she'd seen. Well, maybe not Kenny, but it was pretty hot. The helmet he still had on only added to his sexy allure. Connie wished he would take if off so she could get a look at his face to see if it matched the rest of him. Oh, well, what did it matter? He couldn't be hotter than the man she was waiting for. She headed for the door when the bell rang.

"Yes?" she asked, opening the door.

She watched mesmerized as he removed his helmet. Connie was certain her eyes were threatening to bug out of their sockets as Kenny stood before her, shiny black helmet under his arm and huge smile on his face.

"Hi," he said, a hint of uncertainty in his voice.

"Hi," she stammered, looking from him to the bike he'd just gotten off of.

She glanced down at what she had on and realized she was definitely overdressed.

"I guess I should have mentioned it would be a ride on my bike," he said, his eyes slowly taking in what she had on. "I can always go home and get my car."

It sounded like a great idea to her. After all she'd gone through all this trouble of putting on real clothes. Her make-up was done, and she had managed to do something more with her hair than her normal ponytail. She opened her mouth to say she would wait for him when she glanced up into his eyes and noticed the hint of disappointment in them. She bit her bottom lip as she glanced uncertainly at the bike at her curb. She couldn't help but wonder how many petite bottoms had sat astride it.

"Umm, I've never been on a bike before," she said instead.

She didn't miss the gleam that returned to his eyes at her words. Connie could tell how much he wanted this.

His shoulders, which had been tense moments ago, seemed to be more relaxed. The smile he was gracing her with told her she had made the right decision.

"It's really easy. I'll go slow. I promise."

Kenny's gaze begged her to trust him, and she had to admit she had always thought guys who rode bikes were hot. The thought of being pressed close to his body was exhilarating in itself, but she'd seen women on the backs of bikes, and they had all been small in comparison to her. Was there even enough room on the back of that thing for her? Still wondering about how she was going to fit, Connie stepped back so he could come in as he still stood outside.

"Just let me change clothes real quick," she said and felt her insides flutter at the smile he graced her with.

"I'll wait in the family room," he said, heading in that direction before he stopped and turned around.

Strong arms wrapped around her body, pulling her close.

"I didn't say hello," he said, lowering his head to take her lips in a heated kiss.

As she wrapped her arms around his neck, Connie was glad she'd decided to take a chance on the bike. She only hoped she wouldn't regret her rash decision. No way, her body screamed. If this was the reward she got for trying something new, she'd have to take more chances.

Chapter 12

An hour and a half later, Connie finally caught her breath. She sat astride Kenny's bike outside her house, her arms tightly threaded around his waist. Her upper body pressed tight against his muscled back.

True to his word, he'd started out slow, allowing her time to adjust to being on the bike. Connie didn't know if it was the exhilaration of being on such a powerful machine or the intoxication of being so close to Kenny, but she had felt ready for a little more speed. When they'd stopped at a light while going through the downtown area, she'd given him permission to pick up the pace. Thinking back on it now, Connie realized she probably should have put a little more thought into her decision, especially after he asked for the third time if she was sure. But she'd taken another chance, and man, what a rush. Near the end of the ride, she'd closed her eyes and just lavished in being close to this man who handled the awesome power beneath them with such ease.

Kenny turned the bike off and removed his helmet, placing it on the handle of his bike. She felt his body vibrate before she heard his laughter.

"What's so funny?" she asked.

When he touched her fingers, which were still locked tightly around his waist, she felt her face heat with embarrassment.

"Oh," she said, forcing her fingers to unlock. She moved to lean away from the glorious heat of his body.

Warm fingers closed over hers to hold her in place.

"I hope I didn't scare you so badly you won't ever go for a ride with me again."

Pulling back, Connie removed the helmet from her head and breathed another sigh of relief as cool air kissed her heated scalp. She touched her hair and grimaced when she thought of how unattractive she must look. She ran her fingers through a few times before just giving up.

"No, I asked you to speed up," she said, giving a nervous laugh. "And you did."

She watched as Kenny gracefully swung his leg over the front of the bike. She recalled her own rather awkward mounting and shook her head. She mentally prepared herself for the dismounting, praying for some kind of grace when doing so. But he surprised her by straddling his bike once again. This time facing her. He took the helmet from her hands and placed it carefully on the curb where he'd moved his to at some point.

"I feel as if I should apologize. I should have realized you were still a little uncomfortable when I felt your arms tighten around me," he said, a sheepish expression on his face. "I guess I was kind of hoping it meant you just wanted to be closer to me."

She looked into the uncertain eyes, staring at her and couldn't believe what she was seeing. He doubted himself.

"Kenny, I did want to be close to you. It's one of the reasons why I got on this monster in the first place," she said before she realized how much she was giving away and quickly turned her head.

"Connie."

His deep voice washed over her heightened senses. Taking a deep breath, she slowly raised her eyes to meet his.

"I don't know what this is that's going on between us, but I wanted to share a part of me with you that few know about," he said, edging closer to where she sat at the back of the bike.

She gazed into his shining eyes and couldn't help but wonder if the few who knew of this side of him were all female. How many others had sat astride this powerful machine, arms locked tightly around his waist holding on?

"I must admit it really wasn't that bad once I got the hang of it. I'm sure the other people you've given rides to weren't as challenging as I was," she said, her lashes lowered so he wouldn't see how his next words would affect her.

"Look at me, Connie," Kenny's husky voice commanded softly.

Taking a deep breath, she found the courage to do as he asked. Her breath caught at the emotions she saw tumbling round and round there. The slow smile lifting his lips upwards made her heart skip a beat. He was truly breathtaking to look at.

"I've had my bike for almost three years, and you're the only woman who has ever been on it."

His softly spoken words washed over her, filling every empty hole. Could she believe that? Why would he lie about it?

"I've always wanted to learn how to ride, but I've never had the opportunity before now," she said, licking parched lips.

She saw the way he watched her tongue.

"You're not just saying that, are you?"

"No. I really enjoyed it."

"Are you sure?" He asked, inching a little closer.

"Positive," she whispered, leaning closer to him.

"And you would go out with me again… on the bike?" he asked, stopping just inches from her lips.

"Anytime," she said, closing the distance between them.

A deep sigh moved through her as she closed her eyes and gave herself over to the kiss.

*****

"He's going to hurt her," Brenda said, allowing the curtain to slip from her manicured fingers.

"He seems to like her, and she obviously likes him," Jamie said, still peering shamelessly out the window.

Connie's friends had come home to find a note from her saying she'd gone for a ride with Kenny and would be back later. A few minutes later, Brenda had arrived looking for Connie. They'd been talking about the implications of a second date when they'd heard the sounds of a motorcycle outside. All four had rushed to the windows to see who it was, shocked to find Connie astride on the back.

"I think you're wrong, Brenda," Tammy said, moving from the window and heading for the kitchen.

"You girls obviously don't know anything about guys like Kenny," Brenda said, taking a seat at the kitchen table.

She crossed her slender legs and gazed at Connie's friends.

"And what's to know about him?" Jamie asked, sitting at the table beside her. "He likes Connie, and she likes him. End of story."

"And you don't think it's odd that a guy like Kenny would be interested in our Connie? Come on, Jamie, you can't be that naïve." Brenda gazed at her, a look of disbelief on her face.

"What are you getting at, Brenda? There's no evidence to support anything other than what we've seen so far," Tracy said, coming into the room.

She hadn't been home to meet Kenny on Monday, but her friends had told her all about him as soon as she had walked through the door later that night.

A bored expression graced Brenda's face as she gazed at Tracy.

"Evidence? The evidence is in the way he looks versus the way Connie looks. Not to mention her poor track record with guys in general. No one but me thinks it's odd for a guy who is so hot he could have any woman he wanted to be interested in Constance? Come on, be honest," Brenda said, staring intently at the three women around her.

"We are all aware of Connie's poor judgment calls when it comes to men," Tammy began.

She held her hand up to stop Brenda from interrupting.

"But I don't think this is anywhere close to the same sort of thing. I mean he just seems different to me. Besides Con could use the boost to her self-confidence, which by the way you don't help. Not with all your negativity about her size and what she wears," she finished, giving Brenda an irritated glare.

"Look, Brenda, let it go. You're not gonna find anyone here who thinks Kenny could possibly be using Connie for anything other than what it looks like. And if what I just saw is any indication, I'd like to be used like that my damn self," Tracy said, a smile on her face.

"I second that. Brenda, why don't you go home before Connie gets in here. It'll be easier on all of us and you too in the long run," Jamie said.

Brenda raised an arched eyebrow.

"And why should I? I have a right to try to protect my sister. What kind of sister would I be if I didn't?"

Connie's friends all gave exasperated sighs of disbelief.

"Come off it, Bren. Everyone here knows your only problem with Kenny is he didn't react when you made a pass at him. Plain and simple," Jamie said.

"I did not make a pass at him. If I had, he wouldn't be outside with Constance right now," Brenda said, an indignant tone to her words.

"You most certainly did. And he didn't bat an eye at it. That's why you're all bent out of shape. Hell, I don't think he even recognized who you are," Tammy chimed in.

"Dammit. I miss everything when I work late," Tracy said.

The roommates laughed at the angry expression on Brenda's face. She stood abruptly from the table, her hands on her slender hips.

"I don't know what you are trying to imply, but I take offense. My only concern is that Constance doesn't make a fool of herself over a man who may not be as into her as she's into him," Brenda said. "If none of you plan to do anything about it, then fine. But I will not just stand by and watch her fall on her face."

They watched as Brenda grabbed her purse from the table and walked out of the kitchen, slamming the front door behind her. It only took them seconds to rush from the kitchen to the front windows. They all held their breaths as Connie and Kenny both looked at Brenda.

"Oh, not tonight you don't," Tracy said moving to the front door and opening it. "Good night, Brenda," she yelled.

The look Brenda threw her way before getting into her car may have caused a lesser person to quiver or rethink their actions. But Tracy simply wiggled her fingers at her in dismissal.

"Hey, guys," she called and waved to Connie and Kenny who had embarrassed expressions on their faces.

"Hey, Trace. I'll be inside in a few," Connie said.

"Oh, hon, don't worry about it. You take your time. I just wanted to say goodbye to Brenda," Tracy said, walking back into the house and closing the door behind her before turning to her other two friends.

"She's gonna try to make trouble. I can feel it."

"Hmph, when hasn't she? With a sister like her, I'm surprised Connie's not a basket case and holed up in a padded room by now," Tammy said, running her fingers through her short hair.

"Yeah, she may have had her way in the past, but this time is different," Jamie said, a gleam in her blue eyes and a smile on her face. "I think Connie's finally gotta keeper. I can just feel it."

Tammy and Tracy looked at their friend and hoped she was right. They had all seen the damage done to Connie's self-esteem and confidence through the years. It was past time for her to catch a break.

Chapter 13

Connie woke Wednesday morning, her body aching. It took her a moment to figure out why her thighs were so sore and her arms felt like jell-o. She smiled when memories of last night came back to her. It had been exhilarating. Like nothing she had ever experienced before. The feel of sitting astride Kenny's motorcycle with all that power between her legs. The heat of his body had seeped through her pores as she'd been pressed close to him. And his scent. Oh, she moaned as she remembered how it had drifted across the wind to her nose, threatening to intoxicate her. Easily it had been one of the best dates of her adult life. She had gotten the chance to ride a bike, something she had always wanted to do and spend time with Kenny. Definitely a win – win all the way around.

She stretched her tired body and winced a little as her muscles reacted to the movement. Maybe a hot shower would help. Pushing the covers back, she made herself get up. Despite her Women's Studies professor being kind enough to give them the morning off, she still needed to get to campus. She had a study group at ten, and it was now. ... Glancing at the clock, she was shocked to see it was later than she thought. She was heading for the bathroom when the phone rang. Thinking it might be Kenny, she ran back for it before voice mail picked up. All of her roommates would have been long gone to work.

"Hello?"

"Good morning," Brenda said on the other end.

"Oh, hey," Connie said, trying not to allow her disappointment to show.

"Who did you think it was going to be? Kenny?" Brenda asked on a short laugh.

She was in no mood for this today. She was still flying high from the time she had spent with Kenny last night, and she refused to allow a few petty comments from her sister spoil that.

"What do you want, Brenda? I have to get ready for my study group," she said, heading to her closet to pull out clothes for the day.

"I was just calling to make sure your feet remain on the ground."

Connie paused and glanced down at her feet. She gave her toes a wiggle for good measure. Yeah, they were definitely still on the ground, she thought, fighting back a giggle. She knew what her sister was talking about but refused to get into it this morning with her.

"Excuse me," she finally replied.

"I mean I want to make sure you don't get your hopes up only to have them dashed to the ground again. You know how you like to get worked up, Constance. I'm your sister, and it's my job to protect you."

Connie rolled her eyes. If Brenda thought she was buying the whole "I just want to protect you" act, she needed to think again. In truth, she couldn't fathom the idea of her sister caring one way or the other if she got hurt again. In fact, she would probably prefer it so they could spend some more quality time with Brenda telling her how much of a failure she was at dating and choosing the right man. Then, there would come the not so subtle hints about her weight and the way she dressed being one of the many reasons why she couldn't get a guy and keep him.

"Brenda, I really appreciate your concern, but there's no need for it. I'm okay. My feet are firmly planted on the ground."

Now had she asked her last night, her answer may have been a little different. She'd definitely been floating several feet above ground level after making out with Kenny for an hour outside at her curb, but then she didn't see any reason to share that bit of information with Brenda.

She headed out of her closet, a pair of jeans in her hand she had all but forgotten about along with a t-shirt. She tossed them on the bed. Walking into the bathroom, Connie glanced at her reflection in the mirror. She turned her head to the left and leaned closer. Oh, my gosh. Was that what she thought it was? Her eyes shined brightly as she recalled how she'd acquired that particular love bite. Her lids slid closed as the memory of Kenny's warm lips nuzzling her neck came back to her. When his teeth had first nicked her skin, she had felt a shiver of excitement move through her. Connie placed her hand to her stomach as that same feeling came back again.

"Constance, you are so far out of your element here. Have you ever been out with a guy who falls in Kenny's category of man? Let me answer for you," Brenda continued before she could. "No, you have not. You are not equipped to handle this situation without my help."

"Brenda, I will readily admit to you I have never dated a guy like Kenny before. He's older than any of the guys I've dated, and he's probably got tons more experience than all of them put together."

"Then, as long as we both agree," Brenda interrupted.

"However," Connie continued, staring at her reflection in the mirror. Her brown eyes sparkled brighter than they had yesterday. Her cute as a button face looked a little pretty today. And there was no mistaking the sexiness of the grin slanted across her face. She peered closer at the image staring back at her. Was that really her?

"However," she said again, smiling back at her reflection in the mirror. "I believe I will do just fine on my own."

"There's no way you can hope to handle this situation on your own. Why you're likely to make a fool of yourself by admitting you're not on his level. And goodness knows what other nonsensical things you might say."

Connie couldn't help but laugh at how flustered and upset Brenda sounded. As if Kenny couldn't have figured it out on his own they were from two different worlds. Hell, she had realized it when she had gotten her first look at him in the store.

"No, I will not stand by and allow you to make such amateur mistakes. If you are determined to go after this man, then I can do nothing more than offer my assistance. It's the sisterly thing to do."

Connie was sure she should be offended, but she had to be honest with herself if no one else. She didn't know if she could handle it. The temptation to get carried away in her growing feelings for him was getting increasingly harder to push back. The more time she spent with him and the more things she learned about him only made it worse. She could only imagine it would be more difficult to keep her feet on the ground as time went on. Maybe she could talk to her roommates. They'd had more than their fair share of men experience between them. Of course none of their men had been as hot as Kenny, she thought, feeling the crazy urge to laugh out loud again.

Beep … Beep …

"Brenda, let me call you back. I have to get ready for study group and another call is coming in."

Connie clicked over before her sister could put up a protest.

"Hello?"

"Hey there."

She almost lost her grip on the phone as Kenny's voice came across the phone line.

"Hi," she said again.

"I was prepared to leave you a message. I hope I'm not the reason you're late. I know I kept you out later than planned."

"No, not at all. My professor canceled today's class because our final is next week," she said, moving to sit on the closed toilet seat.

"Oh, okay. I would have felt guilty if I had been the cause of you being late for class. I called to see if you have any plans for tonight? And if you do, if I can possibly convince you to cancel them?"

The uncertainty in his voice caused her heart to flutter and a soft smile broke out on her face. The thought that he wasn't sure if she'd want to see him was nothing short of amazing to her. What woman wouldn't want to spend time with this man?

"No, I don't have any plans," she began before a frown puckered her brow. "Oh, wait. I forgot. One of my study groups is meeting tonight to begin our review for finals."

"How late? I thought perhaps you'd like to go out to dinner. You know on a real date."

It never ceased to amaze her how much he seemed to want to spend time with her. If he kept this up, he might just have her thinking something between them could actually work.

"I'd like that a lot, but I don't get out of my study group until ten, and then I have an early class tomorrow."

"Oh."

She was feeling the same disappointment she could hear in his voice.

"Okay, well, how about tomorrow night instead? That should be enough time for me to make reservations at the jazz club," he suggested.

A smile brightened her face until she realized tomorrow wouldn't work out either.

"No, that's no good either. Another study group til ten. I'm sorry," she said, running her fingers through her hair.

Her plans had been made when she didn't have anyone in her life. Slow down, she told herself. You still technically don't have anyone in your life. Don't go putting the cart before the horse. That's how you get in trouble.

"There's no need to apologize. I remember what it was like when I was in school. Though, it has been a while ago."

"It wasn't that long ago," she muttered.

She'd learned on their first date Kenny hadn't dated anyone her age since he'd been in college himself. The question of why he was bothering with her surfaced again, but she quickly pushed it to the back of her mind. She didn't want to think about that now.

"Yeah, long enough, though."

A deep sigh came across the phone lines, and she got a sinking feeling. Was now when he realized this wouldn't work after all because she didn't have time for him. Connie would bet her life he'd never had a woman not rearrange her schedule to accommodate his, and if she weren't trying so hard not to get ahead of herself, she might have offered to cancel one of her study groups, if not both of them.

"So, it looks like we have a situation here. I want to see you, and you're all booked up for the next how many days?"

Connie tried to decipher if there was any anger or annoyance in his voice. All she could hear was a little frustration, and she could definitely relate to that. She wanted to see him too. Badly. But more than that, she wanted to feel his arms around her again. She wanted to feel his lips on her skin. Oh, hell, she just wanted him.

"Umm, I have study groups tonight and tomorrow night. Both of them are until ten. I don't have any classes or study groups on Friday, but I do have to work."

The sound of Kenny's intercom buzzed through the phone.

"Hang on a second, sweetheart," he said before he began talking to his secretary.

The giddiness she felt over a simple pet name was ridiculous, and she tried to tell herself that, but her body refused to listen to reason.

"Hey, I have to go, but I want to see you. Where's your study group tonight?

"At the library on campus."

"Great. Look, I really gotta run."

"Okay."

"I'll see you later," he said and hung up.

Connie turned off the phone and sat hugging herself on the toilet seat a few moments longer. A small frown marred her brow. What had he meant when he said he'd see her later? She shook it off as nothing. He had been rushing. The bottom line was he wanted to see her. And that's all that was important. Getting up, she caught her reflection in the mirror again and stopped to stare. A smile took shape. Nope, cute wouldn't cut it today. She had definitely upgraded to pretty.

Chapter 14

Oh, thank goodness that's over, Connie thought, packing her books inside her satchel.

"See ya later, Connie," Brad said, waving at her.

She turned to give him a smile and waved goodbye in return. She checked to make sure she had everything before closing her bag and throwing it over her shoulder.

"Hey, Connie, you want me to wait for you," he asked, heading in her direction. "Everybody else has already left."

A soft sigh left her. She would rather he just go ahead, but good manners prevented her from telling him so. Brad had on several occasions asked her out, and she had declined each of them, explaining she believed them to be better as friends. Though at the time he had appeared to have been okay with her decision, it still hadn't prevented him from continuing to ask every so many weeks. She pasted a smile on her face and moved in his direction.

"That's nice of you. Thanks."

"No problem," he said, moving in step beside her as they headed towards the doors.

"So do you have plans for Friday night," he asked, glancing at her sideways as he held the door open for her to exit.

Connie barely held onto the sigh of frustration. Brad really was a nice guy, and to be honest there was no reason in the world she shouldn't have said yes by now. They had been friends for over a year, and he was not a bad looking guy. He came from a good family and for all intents and purposes appeared to be a decent person. But there was just no spark there when she was with him. In the beginning, she had given it serious thought and had almost accepted merely based on all the good things, but he just didn't do it for her. No, decent guys didn't do it for her. She got turned on by guys who looked like they came off the cover of GQ magazine. She forced a smile to her face and was about to give Brad another run down on why it was best if they remained friends when her attention was caught by the sight of a guy who looked a lot like Kenny climbing the library steps in their direction. No way, her rational mind told her. But as the man got closer, her heart stopped because it was him. He was dressed simply in a pair of faded jeans and t-shirt, but she didn't think a guy could look so good.

"Connie, are you okay," Brad asked from beside her.

All she could do was nod because she couldn't tear her gaze away from the man coming towards her with a smile on his face.

"Hey, sweetheart. For a minute I thought I had missed you. It's almost ten-thirty," Kenny said when he reached the top of the stairs.

She saw him glance briefly to where Brad stood beside her. His eyebrow raised in question.

"Our study group ran a little later than we thought it would," she said, finally finding her voice.

At the continued question in his gaze and the confusion on Brad's face, Connie made the required introductions.

"Kenny Jamison, this is Brad Thompson. Brad is in my Mythology class. He was kind enough to wait for me when everyone else had left."

Odd she felt the need to explain Brad's presence beside her.

"What's up, man? Thanks for hanging around and waiting for Connie so she wouldn't have to walk out by herself," Kenny said, his hand outstretched towards Brad.

For a moment, Connie thought Brad was going to refuse the offered hand before he reluctantly took it. He mumbled something about seeing her later. At least, that's what she thought he said before he bounded down the stairs leaving them alone.

"That guy has got it bad for you," Kenny said, his gaze following Brad's retreat.

Connie glanced up at him. There was something in his voice she couldn't quite decipher.

"What are you doing here?" she asked, deciding not to respond to his statement.

His eyes sparkled in the overhanging light of the library.

"I wanted to surprise you," he said, a sheepish expression on his face. "Surprise."

His arms were wide open, offering her what she had been thinking about all evening. She stared at him for a few moments before walking into his open arms.

"For a minute there, I was beginning to wonder if I had done the right thing. You didn't look too happy to see me." Kenny's deep voice rumbled against her ear.

There was something wrong. It was in his voice. Pulling away enough to see his face, her eyes widened in shock and disbelief at what they reflected.

"I didn't know if it was really you when I first saw you coming up the steps."

"Yeah, well, when I saw you come out with lover boy and you didn't look happy to see me, I thought maybe you and he were …. Well, you know."

What was he saying? Her gaze automatically moved to search his, but she found his lids lowered.

"Kenny, surely you aren't jealous of Brad?"

*****

Jealous? Him? Of a guy who was still trying to get what he had already obtained? The thought was ludicrous. Absolutely ridiculous to even consider. Not to mention he had never been jealous of anyone in his life. Men were jealous of him. It had been reflected in Brad's gaze before he had walked off. That's what he was used to. Not the foreign emotions he felt seeing Connie at the library doors with some guy who was looking at her as if he wanted to eat her up. The thought caused him to pause. Could it be possible? Him jealous. Shaking his head to clear the thoughts, he grabbed Connie's hand without saying a word. He pulled her behind him down the steps towards the parking lot, but his thoughts refused to allow him any peace. Jealous. There was no way. His mind quickly ran back over the odd feeling that had run through him when he had gotten his first look at Connie, only to see her standing with Brad. Anger and betrayal mixed with hurt and …. He stopped abruptly in his tracks and turned towards the woman who was causing him to question things about himself and making him feel things he had never felt before. The woman who was causing him to second guess everything about the type of woman he was looking for and the qualities he wanted her to have. Kenny placed both hands on her shoulders and really looked at her. So different from anyone he had ever been interested in before but who surprisingly had more in common with him than the last three women he had dated. There was warmth inside of her that made him melt inside. Her eyes were always open and told him things he bet she didn't even know were being said. It was so refreshing from the cold and calculating women he dated. Women, who in order to get ahead in their careers, had seemed to lose something along the way. Something Connie had. Something that was drawing him in like a moth to flame. Vulnerability. She didn't have all the answers to everything that was going on between them. In fact, she openly admitted to being as confused as he felt. It put them on the same page in this. It made him not feel so bad about the confused state he found himself in lately. He moved his hand to cup her soft cheek. The smile she graced him with made his heart stutter and suddenly it was important for him to make her understand what he was feeling.

"I have been sitting in my car debating on whether or not I should get out for the last twenty minutes. The whole way across the parking lot I ran through all the many reasons why I should turn around and go back home. Then I look up and see you standing outside with a guy who's got his heart in his eyes, and I start to think I might have really made a mistake by coming, yet I tell myself I'm just seeing things. But when you finally see me, the expression on your face is far from the one I had told myself would be there."

Both hands now gripped her shoulders as if to hold her in place in case she decided to run. And who could blame her. The crazy thoughts and emotions running through him had to be showing on his face, and there was no denying the desperation he was feeling. Kenny needed her to understand.

"And, yes, I am jealous of a guy who had the pleasure of spending the last three and a half hours with you while I sat at home pretending to work and trying to convince myself I should stay away the library."

Suddenly finding the whole situation slightly humorous, he gave a short laugh and shook his head.

"You can see how successful I was."

Nerves caused his stomach to churn. In the past, he had preferred to keep his feelings to himself because they were … well, personal. Besides it had been his experience women didn't usually want to know what he was feeling, even when they asked. He glanced over at Connie. He wished she would say something. Anything would be better than the silence. Just then the sounds of soft laughter reached his ears. Well, that wasn't the reaction he had expected.

"Mind sharing what's so funny? I could use a laugh about now."

He couldn't keep the edge from his voice. Here he had just laid his soul bare for this woman, and she had the nerve to laugh at him. There were no doubts now. It had been a mistake coming here. He should have stayed home and dealt with his misery by himself.

"You are," she said, her eyes sparkling with humor.

"I fail to see what I have said or done that is so damned funny."

The smile faded slowly from her face as she looked up at him. He could practically here her mind clicking, going back over all he'd said.

"You were serious? About being jealous of Brad? About worrying about coming here?"

The look of utter disbelief on her face almost had him laughing. That is if he was in the laughing kinda mood.

"Yes, I was," he said, lowering his gaze.

There was an odd ache in his chest, but he fought the need to rub at it. How many women through the years had called him heartless? Well, if they could see him now, he would bet they would enjoy the laugh. The ever cocky and arrogant Kenny Jamison brought down by a college student/gas station attendant. It was unimaginable. It was hard to believe they had only met a few days ago. Yet in that short time, she had turned his world upside down. Made him feel and think about things.

A soft hand caressing the side of his face brought him out of his thoughts. He looked down into her soft brown eyes. The gentle smile lifting her lips made his heart hurt. What was it about this woman that had him tied so tightly in knots?

"I didn't mean to laugh at you, but the thought of you being jealous of Brad ...," she simply shook her head.

"Trust me when I say you have nothing to be jealous of. He's a good guy as a friend, but I don't want to date him. And if that weren't enough, when was the last time you looked in the mirror?"

The scent of her perfume wrapped itself around him. It was a scent he would forever more associate with this woman. Her hands slowly moved up his chest to surround his neck.

"You are gorgeous. There's no way Brad can compete with that," she said before rising on tiptoes to kiss him gently on the lips.

"Not to mention you have some other redeemable qualities."

"Oh, yeah," he said against her lips. "And what would they be because I know plenty of women who would disagree."

Soft laughter came from the woman in his arms.

"Yes, well, I can see how they could say that. You don't exactly allow people to see the real you. The man behind the good looks and the impeccable clothes. Not to mention the air of arrogance that seems to always surround you. It's like a protective shield."

She had his attention now, and he stopped the slow perusal of her neck he had been making while she had been speaking. He lifted his head to gaze deeply into her eyes.

"Go on," he prodded softly.

Kenny tried to tamp down on the need he suddenly felt. He wanted to know what this woman saw in him that others had not. In the past, it had been those very things she had mentioned that had attracted women to him. No one had bothered to look further, or had it been as Connie had suggested? He used the material things to keep women out.

And if that were the case, how had she managed to slip inside?

"There's no secret you are gorgeous. You know and everyone else knows it, too, but you are also kind and smarter than the average bear," she said, laughing softly.

"But more than that, you have a fierce love for your family and friends. In the few short days we've known each other, I have heard the love you have for them in your voice. There's nothing you wouldn't do for them. It makes people wish to be a part of that private group. You have a wonderful sense of humor and great taste in music. There's something about you that draws people to your insides. Or at least it would if you only would allow them time to see the real you."

Connie lowered her head as if embarrassed, and if he were honest, he was a little embarrassed himself. How could someone who had known him for a mere six days possibly see so much in him? More than what Lori had seen in the four months they had been together.

Not knowing what to say, he did what he had wanted to do since seeing her tonight. He lowered his head. He meant for the kiss to be a simple thank you, but at the first touch of his lips on hers, the fire that was always banked when near her ignited and exploded. He pulled her tighter against his hardening body. His hands at her hips held her firmly against his aching groin. This is what he had waited for all day. The need he felt for the woman in his arms was beyond his understanding. He wanted to touch every part of her. He wanted to teach her the true value of who she was. It was important for her to know he saw some of the same qualities in her she saw in him. But more Kenny wanted to erase all those other jerks from her memory. Every guy who had ever done damage to her self-esteem and confidence. All those idiots who prevented her from seeing the true Connie. A soft moan escaped her parted lips, and his tongue moved inside. Connie moved restlessly against him. Hands, that moments ago pulled her closer to him, now stilled her moving hips before he lost complete control and took her right here. Kenny pulled his lips reluctantly away from hers and took a deep breath of air, fighting for control. His body was on fire.

"Connie."

"Hmm," she answered, her head was buried in his neck nibbling.

Damn, she was not making this easy, and the last thing he wanted to do was ask her to stop, but they had to.

"We need to get out of here before they call the police," he said, laughing in an effort to get himself back to normal.

She raised her head. Her eyes were heavy with desire. Desire Kenny felt down to the throbbing dick straining against his jeans.

"Your place or mine?" she asked, gazing up at him with a far off expression on her face.

He saw the shock and embarrassment register on her face when she realized what she had said. If he hadn't been thinking the same exact thing, he might have laughed. But the fire blazing through his blood was no laughing matter. After another quick kiss to her swollen lips, he took her hand and headed across the parking lot.

Despite the late hour there were still a few cars in the library's expansive parking lot, and he realized he had no idea what kind of car she drove.

"Where's your car, sweetheart?"

It seemed to take her a moment to realize where they were.

"It's over there," she said, pointing with her free hand. "Right beside yours."

The low slung bright red sports car caught Kenny by surprise. He vaguely recalled Roger saying her parents were pretty well off. That had been quite an understatement.

"Nice car," he said absently.

"Thanks. My parents got it for me when I graduated from high school with honors," she said, searching inside her satchel for the keys.

He leaned casually against her car and watched her. She seemed to be avoiding looking at him.

"Connie," he began but stopped.

What the hell was he going to say? He felt as if they had both revealed so much tonight already, but she seemed to be embarrassed more so about the passion they had just shared than the words that had been said. He didn't want her to think there was anything wrong with the desire she felt for him ever.

"Kenny, look I'm sorry about what I said a few minutes ago. I don't know what came over me," she said, her gaze still lowered.

He grunted.

"I know what came over you. It's the same thing that came over me."

Tired of watching her fumble around in her bag, he grabbed her hands. Kenny placed two fingers beneath her chin and forced her head up so he could stare into her eyes. What he saw there made him smile. Uncertainty mixed with desire. Yeah, they were both on the same page, and it was refreshing.

"Don't ever doubt how much I want you, Connie. It's all I've thought about since I met you."

Her eyes seemed to be searching his, looking for confirmation of what he was saying. So he stood there with his emotions open so there would be no doubting the truth of his words.

It looked like she was about to say something when his cell phone rang. He gave her an apologetic look before pulling it out of his jeans pocket. Silencing the tone after checking the caller id, he put it back in his pocket. He felt uncomfortable under the weight of her questioning gaze. It was as if she knew it had been a female calling and he felt … well, guilty for it happening while they were together.

Not able to take it any longer, he avoided her gaze by looking down to check his watch.

"Look, I know you have an early class tomorrow," he began.

"Yep, I do," she said a little too quickly. "I guess I had better get going. Besides I'm sure you have things you need to take care of as well."

Kenny didn't miss the accusation in her words, and he felt as if he deserved it.

"Connie," he said, stopping her from opening her car door. "It's not what you think."

The words sounded lame to his ears, but he didn't know what else to say. This was not how he wanted their evening to end, so there was no way he could have this between them.

"Kenny, look, if you needed to answer the phone, all you had to do was do it. Don't try and make me believe your sudden need to leave is for my best interest."

Anger flashed in her eyes for the first time since their meeting, and he paused in what he was about to say. She had a right to be upset with him. He had pulled a typical guy move.

"I'm sorry," he said, holding up his hands in surrender. "You're right. I shouldn't have tried to pass the call off as nothing. But you're wrong if you think I have intentions on returning the call when I leave you."

The look of distrust shining in her eyes brought him back to the reality of what he was dealing with. She had been hurt before by guys who hadn't cared about her feelings. Or bothered to tell her the truth.

"It was my ex-girlfriend, the one who dumped me a few days ago. She's been calling off and on, but I have no desire to talk to her. In my opinion, there's nothing left to say."

It surprised him how dispassionate he truly felt about Lori. She was someone he had shared his life with for over four months. No, he corrected. He hadn't shared his life with her because Lori had only been interested in certain parts. The parts that allowed her to move and network in his professional world. She hadn't been interested in meeting any of his friends. She hadn't been interested in finding out what he liked to do outside of work. But before he allowed the bitterness over the amount of wasted time he had spent on her to fully take root, he realized it had been partially his fault. He hadn't wanted to include her in any portion of his life outside of the comfort zone they had established. But now he wanted something different.

"Oh," Connie said. "I'm sure she has something important to say if she's calling you."

It was her turn to avoid his gaze, but not before he saw misery and distrust enter her eyes. His only thought was to make that look go away.

"There's nothing Lori could possibly have to tell me that I would want to hear. I see no reason to go backwards to try and rekindle what wasn't there to begin with. Besides the road ahead looks so much more inviting. Do you understand what I'm saying to you, Connie?" he asked, a soft smile tilting his lips up.

Confusion clouded her gaze before she shook her head.

"It means, silly girl," he said, taking her face between both his hands. "That I am doing just fine right here. With you. That is, of course, if you'll have me."

Disbelief turned into shock in the blink of an eye as his words seemed to suddenly register. Her jaw grew slack and her mouth opened, but no words came out. Kenny laughed at her response and pulled her to him in a huge bear hug.

"I'll take that to mean you have to think about it."

She nodded against his shoulder, and the smile on his face faltered just a little. Kenny was glad she couldn't see it because the reason behind his doubts had nothing to do with her being a part of his life. If nothing else the time he had spent this afternoon pretending he wasn't thinking about her or what she was doing or who she was doing it with had proved he wanted her in his life. It was the weight of the responsibility he now felt so heavily on his shoulders. What if he wasn't up for the challenge and he became yet another guy who disappointed her? Or worse. What if he hurt her the most?

Chapter 15

Connie threw her backpack on her bed and then fell beside it. She closed her eyes and luxuriated in the peace of being home alone. She allowed the quiet to seep into her pores. It was great living with her best friends, but sometimes it was not the easiest thing. They were lucky that when Tammy's parents had remodeled the house, they had increased the number of bathrooms to match the number of bedrooms. If not, things could have gotten ugly real fast.

She rolled over on her back and stared up at her ceiling, wondering what to do with the free time. It was Thursday afternoon, and her last class of the day and her study group for tonight had been canceled class she wouldn't have minded, but sitting through another three and a half hours of review, she could definitely do without. Last night had been torture. All she had been able to think about was how different her evening would have been had she been with Kenny instead of fifteen of her fellow classmates. But the night hadn't been a total waste. A smile came to her face as she thought back on last night. When she had seen him walking up the library steps towards her. … A giggle escaped, and Connie put her hand over her mouth to contain it, but another burst free. She kept telling herself it was silly to be so excited about seeing another person, but she couldn't help it. Even telling herself to slow down and think this through was having no effect. Somewhere between last night and this morning her common sense had gone on vacation, and she knew exactly the moment it had happened.

"When he asked me to become a part of his life," she whispered to the empty room.

Even now she couldn't believe it. Nor could she believe how she had stood there like some deaf and mute statue as he had practically poured out his heart to her. So much had been running through her head at the time, but she just hadn't been able to put any of it into words. He had seemed to understand and had followed her home when they finally left the library parking lot. They had spent another two hours downstairs in the family room talking and making out. Mostly making out, she thought as another giggle slipped out. Her stomach did flips as the feelings from last night returned in full force. Had it not been for his self-control, she would have let him make love to her right there on the couch with her roommates in the house. And gladly. Her body had been on fire, and she had wanted nothing more than for him to take the decision out of her hands and start peeling clothes from her body. But Kenny had gently put a stop to what they were doing. When insecurities had threatened to make her question why he hadn't followed through and taken her, he had leaned down and whispered softly in her ear, *"When I take you I want only thoughts of me to fill your head. Not thoughts of if your roommates will come down and find us."* Disappointment and frustration had given way to a warm feeling she couldn't explain, but it had put a stop to all the chaos running through her head.

Connie rolled onto her stomach and glanced at the clock. She hadn't talked to him since last night. When she'd tried to reach him between classes today, his secretary had told her he was out. Maybe he was back in the office. Excitement over the thought of spending a night alone with Kenny filled her stomach with butterflies. Just as she was reaching for the phone it rang.

Ring... ring...

"Hello?" she answered.

"Connie?"

"Hey you," she said, rolling onto her back and a smile lifting her lips. Just the person she wanted to talk to.

"I was calling to leave you a message. What are you doing home? I thought you were on campus all day."

"My class and study group for tonight both got canceled. I was just about to call you. "

"You were, were you?"

Thoughts of him had followed her to each of her classes today. Since finding out about her canceled class and study group, she hadn't been able to concentrate on anything except seeing him again.

"Yep, I tried to call you earlier, but your secretary said you were out of the office. I wanted to know if you still maybe wanted to get together tonight."

As soon as the words were out anxiety set in. It was amazing to her that even after he had revealed so much of himself last night she could still question how he felt. But over the years, she had learned to be cautious in revealing too much of how she was feeling.

"So what are you doing tonight?" she asked cautiously.

"Why, what do you have in mind?"

The husky timber of his voice washed over her like a caress against her skin. It sent a thrill through her.

"Well … my roommates all have plans for tonight and … I will be here all alone," she began.

"Don't say another word. I'm there," Kenny interrupted.

Connie checked the clock on her bedside table. It was barely three o'clock. She didn't want to interrupt anything he may have going on at work, but if she said the thought of his being there sooner than later didn't have her body tingling, she would be lying.

"You can come by after work, that's fine."

The sound of rustling papers came across the phone line.

"Shelly, I'll be out of the office for the rest of the day."

She heard him say on the other end of the phone and then came the ding of what sounded like an elevator.

"Where are you going?" she asked, sitting up on the bed.

"To the parking deck. I'll be there in less than an hour."

A smile played around the corners of her mouth. He was leaving work to see her. Though she had tried not to let old doubts affect her, she couldn't deny a fear had always nagged her. A thought always at the back of her mind asking how a man like Kenny could really be interested in her. And the reality was he shouldn't be. After their first date on Monday, things should have ended. He shouldn't have touched her like he had, kissed her like he had. Yet here it was the end of the week, and he was still here. She could no longer ignore the simple truth. He seemed to genuinely want to see her. Spend time with her. Wanted her in his life. How could she possibly continue to ignore that? And when she was with him, she never got the feeling he wanted to be anywhere other than where he was and that was with her. It all had to add up to mean something. Didn't it?

"Kenny," she called his name, a sense of urgency taking over.

A car alarm beeped, and she heard a car door slam. "Yeah."

An engine purred to life in the background.

"Hurry up," she said and hung up.

*****

Kenny tried to calm the fast paced beating of his heart. But it was no use. The thought of being with Connie was all he could think about. Leaving her last night had been one of the toughest things he'd done thus far in his life. All he had wanted to do was drag her to his car and take the short drive to his house where he could show her all the benefits to having a man his age in her life. She had set his blood on boil last night, and it hadn't returned to normal yet.

He glanced at his watch and cursed the traffic in front of him. Didn't these people have anywhere to be? Didn't they have jobs? There were days like today he hated the fact he had chosen to buy a house so far from where he worked. Hitting the interstate, he shifted into fourth and then finally fifth gear. A shiver of pleasure ran through him as he felt the power of the car's engine open up, or was it the thought of having Connie beneath him soon.

Thoughts of her consumed him as he ate up the miles between his office and his home. He still hadn't completely come to terms with what was going on between them. She made him feel things he'd never felt before. Being with her made him question what he had always thought he wanted and needed in a woman to spend the rest of his life with her. He was quickly beginning to realize he had been searching for the wrong things. He'd been looking for things that made for a good business partner not a life partner. He had done more thinking in the last few days about the future course of his personal life than he had in the last several years. And he had come to no conclusions one way or the other. Yet one question refused to go away -

could Connie be the person he had been waiting for? The one who would walk by his side from now until old age. Kenny didn't know, but he was finally prepared to admit to himself that he was willing to find out. With her, he felt as if he could truly be who he was. Not the hotshot businessman other women he had dated seemed to be impressed with. He didn't have to always be "on" for Connie. He could allow the insecurities and uncertainty he felt over what they were doing out in the open without worry over what she would think. All of this had to mean something. Didn't it?

Ten minutes later, Kenny found himself pulling into his garage. He entered his home through the kitchen. He would take a quick shower and then head over to Connie's place for what he hoped would be an afternoon, leading into a long night, of making love. Walking through his house, he glanced around to make sure things were in order. He had no doubts they would end up here.

He had just taken off his shirt and was walking into his bathroom when his doorbell rang. His hand paused on the shower handle thinking he was mistaken. After all, who the hell could it be? No one knew he was at home this early. When the chimes rang through the house again, he, not bothering to put his shirt back on, gave a huge sigh and headed downstairs. He threw the door open wide, not bothering to ask who it was.

"Oh," gasped a surprised Connie, who stood on the other side.

Her hair was pulled up into a ponytail, and she had on another pair of over-sized sweat pants and t-shirt, but a woman had never looked so good to him. He grabbed her arm pulling her inside. Kenny kicked the door closed with a bang and pressed his warm body against hers, effectively pinning her to the door.

"What are you doing here?" he asked, pulling her hair down from its ponytail to run his fingers through it.

He loved her hair. It was soft and thick. He loved the way it felt between his fingers. And it smelled so heavenly, he thought as he buried his nose in her long tresses.

"I thought I saw you pass my house, and I decided to come on over," she said.

Kenny lowered his head; his gaze locked on her parted lips. Her pink tongue slipped out to moisten them, and he felt his body harden painfully. Reaching around her to pull her closer by gripping her full ass in his palms, he moved his lower body against hers. He wanted her to know how she affected him.

"Connie," he began, but stopped when soft hands tentatively began roaming the expanse of his naked back.

She shifted her hips effectively bringing her heated center closer to his throbbing erection. She had to stop, or he wouldn't be able to think. He gripped her moving hips in firm hands in an effort to keep her still.

"Connie."

"Yes," she said, her hands having moved to exploring his naked chest now.

"I want you so bad it hurts. I need to know you feel the same way," he said, gasping when her fingers grazed gently across a hardened nipple.

Her hot mouth lowered to take it within its velvet heat, a rush of fresh desire ran through him, and he thought he would pop through the zipper of his pants.

"Oh, Connie," he groaned.

Her lips moved across his chest, trailing hot kisses to his other nipple.

"Honey, I need you to stop, so we can talk," he said, trying to move her mouth away from his nipple.

"I don't wanna talk. We can talk later if we have to, but for now, I just want you to make love to me," she said, lifting her mouth from his chest.

Unexpected Packages

Kenny had never heard hotter words than the ones just spoken to him. He pulled her towards him and gave her a hard kiss, before pulling her upstairs to his bedroom.

Chapter 16

Connie barely got a glance at the room they were in before she found herself pressed against Kenny's hard chest. His hot mouth quickly descended upon hers stopping all further thought. His tongue thrust itself between her parted lips and made a sweep of the hot cavern of her mouth before retreating. Strong hands moved down her back to tightly grip her full hips, pulling her lower body closer to the hardness of his dick. Moisture leaked from between her legs at the contact. She dragged her mouth from Kenny's in an effort to catch her breath. Dropping her head to his chest, she felt its rapid rise and fall. Stepping back to look into his eyes, she found herself drowning in the emotions swirling through them. The smile he graced her with made her stomach flip and nervousness began to set in. Never had she felt this way about anyone before. From the moment she had first laid eyes on him, she had wanted nothing more than to know what it would feel like to have him touch her.

He slipped her shirt over her head. The look on his face as he took in the lacy scrap of material barely covering her voluptuous lobes made Connie glad she'd spent the extra money. It had been an impulse buy a few weeks ago when she and her girlfriends had been out shopping. At the time, she had thought they would be resigned to remain at the back of her underwear drawer as a reminder of a foolish act. Never could she have imagined she would wear them for a man who oozed sex from his very pores.

A moan slipped pass her parted lips when he cupped her breasts through her bra and pinched her nipples into tight response before lowering his head to take one of her breasts into his hot mouth. Another groan of pleasure escaped her, and she cupped the back of his head to hold it in place. It felt so good she couldn't keep still. Connie moved restlessly against him needing to get closer to his heat. Closer to the hardness she felt throbbing against her leg. The need to feel him everywhere at once threatened to consume her.

A trembling hand moved down the front of the slacks he still wore and gently grazed across the proof of his desire. She wished she had more experience at this so she would know if she was doing it right or not. The soft moan Kenny gave against her nipples when she stroked the long length of him vibrated through her body. Okay, she was on the right track. Connie cupped him through the material of his pants and was awed by the size of him. She didn't have a whole lot to compare him to, but even she realized he was larger than average.

"Oh, god, I want you so bad. Do you feel what you do to me?"

The question came as a hot whisper against her ear. Too full of emotion to speak, all Connie could do was nod. She rolled her head back as lips began to place kisses up and down her neck. Kenny unhooked the front clasps of her bra and pushed it off her shoulders.

"I want …," she began as a fresh assault on her now bare breasts began.

"What do you want, sweetheart? Tell me," he asked around a hard nipple.

Her body was on fire, and she tried to think of what it was she wanted to say, but her lack of experience made it hard to form the words. Or maybe it wasn't her lack of sexual experience. Maybe this is what every woman felt when they had a man who aroused all their senses. The inability to put words into simple sentences.

"Tell me what you want, Connie."

Kenny's soft voice sounded next to her ear. A shiver ran through her body when he tugged her lobe into the hot recesses of his mouth.

"I want to feel you," she managed to whisper.

His head lifted. His eyes were bright with the same desire that was running rampant through her own body. He took a step back and spread his arms wide in invitation.

"I'm all yours. You can touch me as much as you want," he said, walking backwards until he reached the edge of the bed.

Connie walked slowly to where he stood. She lifted her hand, noticing the slight tremble in her fingers. She quickly glanced up to see if he had noticed it as well, but his eyes were closed as he waited for her touch. She ran her hands across his muscular chest taking note his nipples were hard like hers. As her hand slowly explored the many contours of his taut stomach, a small smile lifted her lips as she wondered how many hours he had to spend in the gym to get a body like this. Trembling fingers continued to caress his chest and stomach until she'd worked up enough nerve to reach for the buckle of his pants. After fumbling for what seemed like forever, her fingers suddenly turning to all thumbs, his strong hands covered hers.

"Would you like some help?" his deep voice sounded next to her ear before she felt him brush a soft kiss against her temple.

Connie kept her head lowered in embarrassment. She removed her hands from his buckle and stood there, staring down at his expensive loafers and then her own battered sneakers. She looked from his flat stomach to her own less than perfectly flat one. Feelings of inadequacy and insecurities bombarded her. Had his eyes been closed because he was anticipating her touch or had they been closed because he didn't want to see her flabby body? No, she tried to tell herself. That's not why his eyes were closed. He was the one who had undressed her. He knew it wasn't perfect. Not like his. Strong fingers lifted her chin until she was staring into concerned eyes. Surprised to find tears burning the backs of her eyes, Connie turned away from his penetrating gaze and put some distance between them. She fought to control the chaos running through her. Her body shook with her efforts. She picked up her t-shirt and pulled it over her head to cover herself.

"What's wrong, Connie? The last thing I want to do is rush you."

She ran her fingers through her hair and tried to calm down. Memories she thought she'd gotten over were at the forefront of her mind.

"Connie," he called.

She felt his presence behind her. His body was so solid behind her. She allowed herself the weakness of leaning against him. But just for a moment she told herself. She'd break away any minute now.

"Talk to me. I thought you wanted this as much as I did. If I was wrong, tell me."

If only it were that simple. But as the thoughts whirled around in her head, they seemed silly to think about, yet she couldn't stop. What if he didn't enjoy having sex with her? What if he found her body as repulsive as she sometimes did? Would he still want to be with her afterwards? Whether it was good or not.

Kenny wrapped her within his embrace from behind and whispered soft words in her ear. It was all too much.

How pathetic was she? Brenda had been right. She wasn't woman enough to hold a man like this. Hot tears slipped down her cheeks. Connie raised her hand to wipe them away before he could see them when she felt herself being turned.

"Sweetheart, if you don't tell me what's wrong, how will I know how to fix it. I don't want to rush you into something you're not ready for just because my dick is about to burst at the seams," he said, laughing softly while brushing away a tear with his thumb.

Genuine concern shined in his eyes and made her feel worse.

"The thought of me naked doesn't turn you off?"

As soon as the words left her lips, she instantly wished she could take them back. And when she looked up and saw the strange look on Kenny's face, she wanted to sink through the floor.

"Never mind. Forget I asked. I think I'll go home now... and die," she said, pulling out of his grip and heading for the door.

She didn't make it very far before she was hauled back against his hardened body. She felt his hot breath next to her ear. Her body tensed.

"When I think about all those idiots who have caused you to doubt yourself, I could wring their necks with pleasure."

Connie could hear the anger in his voice.

"You asked me if your body turned me off. Basically, what you want to know is if I really want to have sex with you."

He paused a moment before shaking his head.

"I have wanted you since the first night I saw you. You were standing there frowning at me, and I could practically feel the drool running down my chin," he said, laughing.

"It was so obvious you weren't interested in anything I had to say, and all I could do was imagine how your breasts would feel in my hands. In my mouth."

Kenny emphasized his words by taking her mounds now between his large hands and squeezing.

"Hmm," he sighed. "They feel as good as I imagined they would. Over the last week as I've gotten to know you, my desire for you has only intensified."

Connie tried to think pass the feel of those hands caressing her breasts, but it was difficult.

"I don't have the experience you have, Kenny. I can count all the guys I've been with on one hand," she replied. "And still have fingers left."

He turned her around to face him, the evidence of his desire pressed tightly against her stomach.

"I love the fact you haven't slept with a lot of guys. That means you think I'm special enough to be one of the few. In fact, I should be the one who's nervous about not living up to your expectations."

What was he saying? How could he not live up to her expectations? Her body had been on fire for him since he had first walked into the store. All he had to do was stroke her between her legs now and she would explode into a thousand pieces.

"Are you nervous," she asked in a whisper.

Instead of answering, he took her hand and placed it to his chest. The erratic beating of his heart pounded strongly against the palm of her hand refused to be denied.

"This is what you do to me. It's been a long time since I've been concerned about my ability to pleasure the woman I was with," he said, his breathing coming out ragged.

Next, he placed her hand over his hardened dick.

"Feel how you affect me, Connie. I want this more than I can possibly tell you. But the choice is yours. If you say we wait, then we wait until you're ready."

Never before had she felt so much power over a man. His dick swelled and throbbed against her hand. If any doubt remained in her mind to his wanting to have sex with her, it was now completely gone.

She wanted this. She wanted him. And whatever happened tomorrow or the next day happened. But for tonight, she was going to accept what he was offering. Stepping away from him, she took a deep breath before pulling her shirt over her head and throwing it behind her. Reaching for his belt buckle, she managed to undo his pants with minimal fumbling and pushed them down. She glanced down at the evidence of his arousal when it thrust forward for release against the front of navy blue silk boxers.

"I had you pegged for briefs," she said on a nervous laugh.

"Yeah, well, I find that boxers allow for easier removal," he said before lowering them over his lean hips and down his strong muscular legs.

Kenny quickly stepped out of his clothes until he stood naked in front of her. He reached for her hand, pulling her towards the bed.

"I'm only gonna be able to make this offer one more time because once I start touching you, I don't think I can stop," he said before she placed a finger to his lips to silence his words.

Connie reached for her pants and pushed them down, taking her panties with them, until she stood naked in front of him as well. For the moment all self-doubt was gone as heat spread through her body, making a pit stop between her legs. She felt her clit begin to throb with unfulfilled need.

"All I want is to feel you inside me," she said.

That was all the invitation he seemed to need. He pulled her to him, and they both fell backwards onto the bed. She had no idea how he ended up on top, but as he began placing hot kisses across her full breasts, she found it wasn't important. She spread her legs to make room for the thigh he pressed against her. Moving restlessly against it, she moaned as her whole body began to throb in need.

"My god, Connie, I wanted to take my time, but I don't think I can last," he said, moving to suckle her breasts.

"I don't wanna wait," she said, trying to catch her breath.

Kenny moved his hand down between her legs and stroked her gently before thrusting a finger inside her. There was some discomfort, but it was to be expected. It had been a long time since anything had been inside of her, and his finger was large, yet she found it wasn't enough. She wanted and needed more.

"Kenny, please don't tease me," she begged. "I want you inside me now."

Another finger joined the first, and he stroked in and out stretching her further.

"I feel the same way, sweetheart, but you are so very tight," he said through clenched teeth. "I don't want to hurt you, so I have to make sure ...."

Just then his fingers grazed against a spot deep inside her, and her hips came off the bed.

"Oh, yeah ... I have to make sure you're ready," he said against her ear.

Again his fingers hit that spot, and her stomach muscles tightened. Connie almost didn't notice when the third finger joined the others and began thrusting in and out of her slowly at first before picking up speed. She opened her mouth to tell him she was about to cum, but no words came out as her orgasm hit her full on. Her hips thrust against the fingers still deep within her, riding them and drenching them in her juices.

"Oh, good, I could watch you cum all day," Kenny said, removing his fingers.

He settled his body fully between her legs, his hard dick pressing against her hot opening.

"Now I think you're ready," he said before thrusting slowly into her aching pussy.

A soft sigh of pleasure escaped pass her parted lips, and she closed her eyes tightly. Oh, this was nothing like the dildos she had used over the past several months to quench the ache. They had not come close to giving her the feelings moving through her body now as Kenny began slowly thrusting in and out of her pussy. It was like heaven. She opened her mouth to tell him how good it felt, but no words would come out. Even the scream of pleasure she wanted to release was lodged at the back of her throat. Jagged breathing sounded next to her ear as the speed of his thrusts increased. Deeper and harder into her moist center. Her muscles tightened around him, wanting to keep him inside of her for as long as she could but knowing that only when he pulled out could she obtain that wonderful feeling again. It was like a game their bodies were playing. When he entered her again she opened herself wide for his entry, but her cunt muscles tightened once more, not wanting him to leave the confines of her heat.

"Oh, baby, your pussy is so tight," he breathed against her neck. "I don't know how much longer I can hold on."

She was so close to her orgasm, and she didn't want it prolonged. She'd already had to wait to be beneath him, his strong, powerful dick filling all of her crevices.

"Harder, Kenny. I want it harder," she said, reaching to grab his ass and pull him closer to her.

She saw him rise up on his arms and look down at her, a slanted grin on his face.

"Your wish is my command."

He pulled out until only the large head of him remained inside of her opening. Kenny thrust his hips forward in a powerful stroke until the tip of his dick hit the back wall of her cunt. Connie arched her back as pleasure and pain shot through her. She'd never been filled like this before. Each thrust of his powerful hips brought her closer to the edge until she felt a tightening in her stomach. She welcomed the feelings as they washed over her now.

"Oh, Kenny, I'm gonna cum," she screamed, closing her eyes tight against the pleasure moving through her.

She was only vaguely aware of Kenny's shout of pleasure as liquid heat shot from his dick mixing with her own release. As the sensations moved over her, she tried to catch her breath but couldn't. Hot liquid slipped from inside of her as he continued to move in and out of her, pumping harder and faster until her body tensed suddenly. She couldn't believe it as another more powerful orgasm was pulled from her. Her eyes were closed tight against the pleasure. It was as if she were suspended somewhere above her body, watching it jerk about on the bed until finally she was able to relax. Kenny's body slumped down upon her, and she luxuriated in the feel of it. Her arms wrapped around his sweat covered back. A soft kiss landed on her neck before his head lifted and wonder filled eyes stared down at her. Connie didn't know what to say or if she should say anything at all. Her body still tingled from the pleasure she'd just experienced at the hands of the man above her. She didn't know how long this was going to last, but she had to admit there were definite advantages to stepping outside of her normal comfort zone.

Chapter 17

Kenny laid there, his arms wrapped around Connie's naked body. The throbbing in his dick belied the fact they had already made love several times. How could he want her again and so soon after the last time? Barely an hour had passed. But the tee-peed covers told of his body's readiness and apparent need for the woman lying warm beside him.

Connie stirred, her body brushed against his throbbing dick. His mind was full of what he wanted to do to her still and of what they had already done. He wanted her awake and writhing beneath him in passion, her body so slick with need and want he could drown in her juices. A groan of frustration left him. This was not where his thoughts should be if he wanted to allow her to rest.

Kenny glanced at the clock on the nightstand. It was close to midnight, and he had a hectic day ahead of him tomorrow. Meetings that had been rescheduled from Monday when he had left early and surely some things he would have to take care of from today. As he mentally reviewed his calendar, he felt his body relax finally until tension of another kind filled him. Thinking of his calendar reminded him that his friend, Marcus, was throwing a party in a few weeks. The question of whether or not he was ready for his relationship with Connie to become public knowledge flitted across his mind. How would his friends react to her? Kenny could imagine the looks of disbelief. They were used to seeing him with a certain type of woman, and admittedly, Connie was not that kind of woman. Then, what are you doing with her? The question loomed over his head like a thunder cloud following him about.

Kenny shifted on the bed under the uncomfortable weight of the questions moving around in his head. He pulled his arm carefully from under Connie's softly snoring body. After the way he'd gone at her tonight, he wasn't surprised when she barely stirred. He brushed the hair back from her forehead. His brain was telling him all the reasons why he shouldn't have any feelings for this woman. But his heart was telling his brain it was a liar.

He moved slowly to a sitting position, his head in his hands as he tried to fight the confusion he was feeling. There was no denying she was not his typical kind of woman. He knew it, and she knew it. He glanced back at her sleeping form. Yet, here she was in his bed where he wanted her to stay. He grabbed a pair of pajama bottoms from his dresser and pulled them on before heading downstairs.

His thoughts weighed heavy on his shoulders as he sat down with a bottle of water at the counter. Things were so jumbled up inside of him that he realized he needed to talk this thing through, but who could he call? Never mind the late hour, he knew that none of his friends would understand. He laughed as he thought of what their advice would be – fuck her until you get over it. Yeah, that would help a lot. Not. Kenny didn't even know why he was delaying the inevitable. There was really only one person he knew for certain he could count on to give it to him straight.

"Hello," the female voice answered on the other end of the phone.

"What are you still doing up? Do you know how late it is?" He asked, feeling instantly better at the sound of her voice.

Soft laughter rang through from the other end, and it brought a smile to his face.

"Why are you calling me after midnight if you didn't think I'd still be up?"

It was Kenny's turn to laugh.

"I need to talk to you about something, Mom."

"What's wrong, honey? Are you okay?"

His mother's tone had lost all hints of humor.

"Yeah, I'm fine, but I need to talk to you about this woman I met."

Nothing could have prepared him for his mother's laughter. He allowed her a few minutes for the shock to apparently wear off, but when the merriment continued, it began to grate on his nerves a little.

"Mom, I'm serious here."

"I'm sorry, honey, but you caught me off guard," his mother said, clearing her throat. "I'm glad you called me. Really, I am."

Amusement still sounded in her voice.

"Yeah, well, right now I'm rethinking it."

"Oh, stop being dramatic. From the day you realized you could get any woman you set your mind on, you've never asked anyone for advice on women. Especially me. I think you were about ten when the realization hit."

Kenny smiled in spite of himself. She was right. His interaction with women had always been simple in the past. He saw one he liked, he approached, smiled that smile all women could interpret as interest and he was in. But

Connie, she had been the exception to the rule. He approached, and she backed away. He smiled, and she frowned.

"Yeah, well, this one is different."

"And how many times have I heard that one before," his mother asked.

The soft laughter still coming from his mother caused his brow to crease in a deeper frown. He and his mother had always been able to talk freely about everything no matter how sensitive the topic. When he had first decided to have sex, it had been his mother instead of his father he had gone to and told what he was planning. His mother had sat him down, explaining his responsibilities as a man. It was up to him to protect himself and the woman he was with. Protection … Oh God, how could he have been so stupid? What had he been thinking? Hmph, that was a stupid question.

"Oh, Mom, I just messed up big time."

When Connie had turned to him finally having come to grips with whatever demons had been causing her concerns, he'd been so ready. It had taken all of his willpower not to cum just at the smell of her arousal.

"Honey, I find that hard to believe. But why don't you tell me about it," his mother said, her calm and soothing voice coming through the phone; all laughter was now gone from her voice.

Embarrassment caused his face to burn with heat as he explained. After quickly wrapping up his oversight, he told his mother about Connie. When he explained how they had met and how against their initial date she had been, his mother's laughter had again sounded through the phone.

"Honey, mistakes can happen when emotions get involved. Things move fast and sometimes we just follow the flow. I'm sure your young lady has taken precautions of her own. If she's as smart as you seem to think she is, then she wouldn't leave something as important as birth control solely in the hands of a man."

Despite knowing what his mother said was probably true, jealousy and possessiveness ran through his veins. The thought of his Connie having sex with other men was not something he wanted to think about. Ever.

"Especially since she wasn't the least bit taken with your other personality, I can see she's quite intelligent. So what's the problem?"

It was that very question that had him downstairs instead of lying in bed beside Connie. It was why he was on the phone after midnight talking to his mother of all people. Kenny had always thought when it came to finding the woman he would settle down with it would be someone more like him. A woman with confidence and already established in her career. Someone who knew how to handle themselves in the world in which he lived. Hmph, someone who was closer to his own age.

"She's younger than me," he blurted out.

"Interesting. How much younger?" his mother asked.

"She'll turn twenty-two in a few months," Kenny answered absently, his mind moving to thoughts of what he could do to help her celebrate.

"Well, that's definitely a change. It's also one way to keep you young."

"Did I mention she's still in college?"

"Really. What's she majoring in?"

"English. But she'd really like to go into journalism."

"Well, she and your father will get along famously," his mother replied simply.

Kenny nodded in agreement, not that his mother could see. His father had been an English professor at the local college where Connie now attended before he retired a few years ago. He still guest lectured from time to time for the English department. He would have to remember to ask if she knew him.

"Yeah, I'm sure they will," he replied, confused over his conflicting thoughts.

"Did I mention she's not as skinny as the women I normally date?"

"Mmm hmm, you did. Did I ever tell you that I was the first black woman your father ever looked at twice, and at a whopping size sixteen, I was also the heaviest woman he had ever dated?" His mother asked casually.

Kenny thought back on the way he had seen his father look at his mother through the years. Never had he suspected his father had liked his women smaller or lighter for that matter. Not once could he ever recall him looking twice at another woman even when his mother had not been around.

"Honey, listen to me. I have watched you over the last several years date a countless number of women and not one of them would I deem worthy of my son. Now, it's not abnormal for a mother to think her son is the best thing since sliced bread," she said, laughing. "What's rare is that I can actually say it's true of all my boys."

Kenny couldn't help but laugh. His mother was proud of her three sons and never failed to let anyone who would listen know of their many accomplishments.

"My biggest fear has always been you would marry someone for all the wrong reasons. And pardon me for saying so, but you don't marry someone because they look good on your arm or because they can talk business as well as the next man or to give you a different circle to network in."

It was the first time he had heard how displeased his mother was with the way he was living his life, and it caught him off guard. They had always been close, and he would have expected her to tell him if he were doing something she disapproved of.

"Why didn't you ever tell me any of this before now?"

"When have I ever meddled in your life? Your father and I raised all our boys to know right from wrong, good from bad. And hopefully we have given you an idea of what a good, fulfilling relationship looks like. No matter how many times I've wanted to pull you to the side and question your choices, I held my peace. All because I knew deep down inside when it came to choosing the woman you would spend the rest of your life with, you would make the right choice. Was I wrong?"

A heavy sigh moved through him.

"I don't know, Mom. This has been the oddest week of my life. It's almost like an out of body experience."

"Don't you think you're being just a tad bit melodramatic, Kenneth?"

"Mom, you just don't understand. It's like I'm somewhere watching my body do things that last week I never would have thought about. If someone had told me last week …. Hell, if someone had told me on Friday morning that I would meet a full-figured, twenty-something, college student at a gas station who would make me forget all women but her, I'd have asked what they were smoking. Since meeting Connie, she's all I think about. And she's so far removed from all the other women I've been involved with," Kenny said, running his fingers through his wavy hair.

He absently fingered his hair's length. It was past time for a haircut. Maybe he'd let it grow out a little? He'd been thinking of changing it for a while but hadn't because Lori had told him she preferred it short. Maybe that wasn't the only change he was ready for in his life.

"Yes, you've mentioned she's different from any other woman you've been involved with. But is that such a bad thing?"

Kenny paused. Well, was it? He couldn't deny he enjoyed being with her. And he was almost used to the funny feeling he got in the pit of his stomach when he knew he was going to see her.

"And you're sure it's not just a sex thing? I hate to say this, but men since the beginning of time have confused true feelings with lust. You wouldn't be the first."

By now Kenny knew he should be used to his mother's frank nature, but there were times like now when it still caught him off guard. He forced his jaw to close and focused on what she had asked him. Could she really be serious? To think he didn't know what he was feeling? That he could mistake the odd emotions rolling around inside for … for lust? He thought she knew him better than that.

"I know what lust feels like. And just for the record, I can get sex anywhere and from anyone. How could you ask me that, Mom?"

"Because I'm sure it's one of the many questions you've been asking yourself in an attempt to dispel what you're feeling for this young woman. A woman who obviously has you just a little bit out of sorts," his mother said softly.

Any anger Kenny might have been feeling drained from his body.

"How did you know?"

His mother simply laughed.

"Sweetheart, I'm your mother. I know everything," she said, laughing softly into the phone.

Well, he wasn't sure about her knowledge of everything, but she sure did know him. In fact, he would dare say she knew him better than anyone else.

"Now when do I get to meet your young lady?"

He tossed the question about in his brain for a few, testing it out to see how it felt. And for the first time, he realized he actually wanted his mother to meet someone he was dating. But could he call what he and Connie were doing dating? They hadn't technically gone out on one real date. In fact, he hadn't done any of the things he normally did to get a woman interested in him. Hell, there were good reasons for that too. He'd determined pretty early on that none of the things he normally did to impress women would work. The powerful people he dealt with and called his friends wouldn't impress her. She was still in college, so networking and social climbing weren't high on her list of priorities. She'd let him know the first night that fancy restaurants weren't her thing. And based upon what he'd seen of her wardrobe thus far, he could guess expensive gifts of clothes or jewelry wouldn't win him any brownie points either. So what had he been left with? Being himself? Kenny was surprised he'd gotten as far as he had.

"I'd like for you to meet her. But I think I'd better figure out where I want this to go first. Don't you think?"

"Kenneth Anderson Jamison, you have never been uncertain of the direction you wanted to go since the day you were born. I think you came out planning your attack on the world. Honey, when we are faced with new challenges that require us to step outside of our comfort zone, our first instinct is always to run. There's a part of you telling you to run back to what you're familiar with. And it'd be so easy to listen to that part."

Who was she telling? Kenny couldn't count the number of times he'd almost ran screaming back for the safety of the Loris of the world in the past few days. It was easier on his ego and his emotions, which hadn't worked this much in he didn't know how long.

"But when we do, we cheat ourselves out of so much. Imagine if you had listened to that voice telling you Connie wasn't your type and had just walked away. You would never have felt the excitement of getting to know somebody new and knowing they like you because of who you are. The man and not the career or the car or the house. But for Kenneth. How long has it been since you could say that you got a woman in your bed simply for being yourself?"

A slow smile came to his face. This was why he had called her.

"Now when do I get to meet Connie? We'll invite your brothers. That way she can meet the whole family at once. For your sake, I hope after being charmed by your brothers, she still wants you."

Kenny laughed at his mother's words.

"They learned from the best," he said. "Look, Mom, I'm gonna let you get some rest, and I'm gonna head off to bed."

There was a pause on the line, and he thought for a moment his mother was going to read him the riot act for not answering her question.

"Okay, I know you need your rest but allow me to say this one last thing. I've learned that love can come in the most unexpected packages. It's up to us to decide if we want to open the package and see the true beauty inside or if we want to take it at face value for its questionable wrapping."

Kenny paused, not sure he knew what his mother was talking about or was it just that he was unwilling to admit she was right on target.

"Yes, Mother, I will take that into consideration."

He glanced at the clock over the stove. It was almost one o'clock.

"I'll call you later this weekend. Tell Dad I love him."

"I will, honey, and we love you, too," she said and hung up.

Kenny headed back upstairs. He paused in the doorway of his bedroom and took in the sight of Connie in his bed. There was no explanation for the peace he felt just watching her sleep. Any earlier misguided thoughts he may have had of giving her up to someone were dismissed. Maybe he was being selfish. But he knew in the time it took him to walk from his bedroom door to his bed, he'd never find anyone better for him.

He slowly slipped back under the covers and felt her stir.

"Where were you?" she asked, her voice husky with sleep.

He pulled her closer to him until her head rested on his chest close to his heart, where she'd already begun making a place for herself.

"I was downstairs getting something to drink."

"I thought you had run off."

A soft laugh came from her as she burrowed deeper into his arms.

"You couldn't run me off if you tried," he said, kissing the top of her head.

A soft hand brushed across his groin, and he felt his body's immediate response.

"Hmm, good. Why do you have these on?" she asked, pulling at his pajama bottoms.

Without answering, he got out of bed and quickly stripped them from his body. Connie's mouth opened slightly, and he saw the pink tip of her tongue move across her lips. His body began to throb. Kenny longed to be buried between her luscious lips. And right now, he wasn't too picky as to which set. He noticed the slight tremble in the hand reaching out to touch his straining dick, and it took everything for him to stand there. When she began to stroke him around the hardened head, the air left his lungs, and he couldn't contain his groan of pleasure. Connie didn't allow him time to catch his breath before she moved her whole hand up and down the length of his dick. She got to her knees, spreading them wide on the bed to help her keep her balance. Kenny glanced down and could see the dewy moisture glistening on the hairs between her legs. His dick hardened further.

"Ahh, Connie," he breathed as her hot mouth closed around his swollen head.

Kenny moved his hand to the back of her head to hold her in place as she began swirling her tongue around the tip. The hot wetness of her mouth felt almost as good as it did when he was balls deep in her tight pussy. No, there was definitely no way he was giving this up. In fact, he needed to begin making plans on how to keep her.

Chapter 18

"So no class today, right," Kenny asked, getting up from the counter, empty plate in one hand and coffee cup in the other.

Connie had surprised him by coming downstairs to make breakfast while he had been in the shower.

"I normally only have one class on Fridays in the afternoon. My journalism class. But since I turned in my paper already, I'm free all day until I go to work tonight," she said, clearing the counter of her plate and juice glass.

Sitting back down at the counter with a fresh cup of coffee in his hand, he marveled at how right she looked moving around in his kitchen. She was dressed in one of her oversized t-shirts that fell just above her thighs and nothing else. The glimpses of panties she kept giving him were making him hard. By the time he had gotten up, she had already showered. He hadn't made any comments on it, but he wished she would have waited so they could have showered together. Granted it would have taken longer to get clean, but oh, what fun it would have been. He hid the smile on his face behind his coffee cup.

"So what time do you go in tonight?"

"Roger asked me last weekend if I would be willing to come in at midnight tonight, but my normal hours are nine to three in the morning."

He made a face.

"Okay, so that means you get off at what time?"

It was beyond his realm of understanding why anyone would have taken a job with hours like those. Especially when it was obvious she didn't need the money. He was strongly considering calling Roger up and asking him to fire Connie.

"Six."

Six o'clock in the morning. That was a whole night he could spend making love to her until she couldn't walk straight. What a waste of a good night.

"Why did you take this job?"

She walked over and kissed him lightly on the forehead.

"Because I don't have a life," she said, a smile on her face.

"Well, that was last week. This a whole new week," he said, grabbing her around her waist and pulling her against his body. "And you have a man who would like to spend some time with you. Next week you'll be bogged down in finals and any time I take away from your studies will cause me to be consumed by tremendous amounts of guilt."

Connie laughed as he'd wanted her to, but his own laughter quickly died when she began pressing kisses against his neck. Flames licked at his insides as the desire that had been banked came slowly to life.

"So what say I give Roger a call and see if he would be willing to let you off this weekend so we can maybe go on a real date and spend some quality time together?"

As the slow trail of moisture moving down his neck to his shoulder grew in intensity, Kenny realized he was only half joking. If she gave him any indication she was on board with his plans, he would be on the phone so fast.

"You're kidding right?" she asked him, leaning away from him slightly.

He leaned over and nibbled on her neck. His hands moved slowly down her thighs before slipping beneath the short hem of her shirt where they cupped her large ass and squeezed.

"Oh, no, I'm very serious."

Suddenly his arms were empty. His head popped up, hazel eyes glittering with unchecked desire.

"Look, I know my job is not the end all be all of jobs and next to yours, it's nothing. But it's a responsibility I have taken on, and I have no intentions of letting you pull any kind of strings just because my having it is an inconvenience to you."

The disbelief in Connie's eyes was as apparent as her anger. Okay, so obviously that hadn't gone over well. His mind tried to think past his desire for some way to make this right. But her anger seemed to only stroke the fires.

"Okay, forget I suggested it," he said, getting up slowly, mindful of his aroused state.

Kenny walked over to where she leaned against the opposite counter, arms folded across her ample chest. It amazed him just how hot he had gotten when she had turned to him with fire shooting out of her eyes? Even now as the gaze that watched him hardened, his dick swelled against his slacks.

"Connie, I'm sorry. I didn't mean to imply your job is less important than mine. If it makes you feel any better, how about we both skip work today. We can stay here and play hooky," he said, pulling her reluctant body into his strong embrace. "We'll make a little nooky. Come on, don't be mad at me. I don't want our first fight to be over something like this."

Kenny almost backed off when he saw her raised eyebrow at his comment. Instead he decided to live dangerously. He alternated between nibbling on her earlobe and whispering obscenities about what he wanted to do with her into her ear until he heard her giggle.

"Okay. I'm sorry too. I may have overreacted," she said, her breath coming out in short gasps.

Her hands caressed his strong arms through the material of his shirt.

"It's okay. It was my fault. I shouldn't have suggested it. But since I have, how about that hooky nooky day?" he asked, only half kidding.

There were a ton of things on his calendar for today, but he realized if it meant he could spend more time with this woman, he would push it all back until next week. He could start his weekend early. That was something he hadn't done in a very long time. More often than not, he found himself starting his work week on Sunday because of his work load. And his load hadn't changed at all in the week he'd known Connie. It just didn't seem to be the most important thing in his life anymore.

"After you gave me an outline of your day not thirty minutes ago? No way," she said, moving over to the counter to pour herself a cup of coffee.

A deep sigh left his body.

"But I want to see you this weekend."

Was that him whining like some two-year-old kid who wasn't getting his way? Yes, it was, and oddly enough he didn't care.

"Well, it's good for you I don't require a lot of sleep," she said, looking at him and winking. "You can come over after you get off. Maybe we can grab a bite to eat before I have to go to work."

His thoughts immediately moved to what he had on his calendar for the afternoon. If he rescheduled some things to next week, he might be able to get off a little early. Never mind the fact he had already skipped out on work twice this week. There had to be something that could be rescheduled. He made a mental note to ask Shelly about it when he got to the office.

"Okay, I'll work something out," he said, glancing at his watch.

Connie simply laughed and moved to give him a brief kiss on his lips.

"I'm sure you will. I don't work on Sundays at all. So if nothing else, we can spend the day together if you want."

Kenny raised his eyebrow. He knew her well enough now to recognize she wasn't sure of how he'd react to her comment. He tipped her chin up so his gaze locked with hers.

"I very much want to spend every possible minute with you, Constance Banks."

He pulled her closer to him and buried his nose in her neck and inhaled. She'd apparently come prepared last night to spend the night because she smelled of jasmine, and he knew he didn't have that particular scent in his bathroom. He took another deep breath.

"Mmm, you smell good enough to eat," he said, nibbling at the side of her neck.

His body hardened further when he felt her hand brush the front of his pants.

"You did that last night," she said, laughing at him.

Kenny's laugh came out a little strained. But it was hard to laugh and try to breath at the same time with her squeezing his dick. He grabbed her ass in his hands and pulled her closer. A finger slipped inside the material of her panties, and he stroked between the crease of her ass, moving slowly around her puckered brown hole before exploring a little further to the ultimate prize. He wondered if one day she'd allow him to initiate her into the ways of anal sex. He had played with it repeatedly last night during their lovemaking, and she had seemed to enjoy it.

"I can't get enough of a good thing," he said, pushing his finger in hard.

Connie gasped, and her head fell forward on his shoulder. He kissed her temple before removing his finger from her panties to cup her full breasts through her shirt. He pinched the nipples through the material.

"You're gonna be late for work," she said, moving her hand to his tie and pulling it loose.

Her fingers worked quickly to unbutton his shirt, so she could press kisses across his bare chest. Kenny couldn't believe this was the same woman who had fumbled through unbuckling his pants last night. He had watched the change come over her in the wee hours of the morning when finally she had gotten up the nerve to explore his body. Taking her time, kissing and licking every inch of him. Trying to discover what excited him. In all his years of having sex never had a woman paid so much attention to his pleasure before. Always in the past, they had only been concerned about their own needs. Connie's fingers gently brushed against his swelling dick before they squeezed him through his slacks. Kenny took a deep breath in. No, this was definitely a different woman, and he was absolutely going to be late. He tried to think of what his first appointment of the day was, but he couldn't think pass her hot mouth pressing against his dick. But he needed to think. His first appointment…what was it. His boxers were lowered carefully over his extended flesh. What was his first appointment and could he skip it? When her mouth engulfed the head of his dick, he gave up. It was no use. The only thing he could bring to mind was the way she was moving along the length of him. The way her tongue was swirling around the swollen head of his dick before her throat relaxed and she took him further down than she had last night. His head fell back, and he gripped the edge of the counter at his back.

"Oh, god, Connie, I'm gonna cum," he said, surprised at how close he was to his orgasm already.

Her mouth tightened on him like a vice, and he went over the edge. His hot load shot from his dick, and he couldn't control it as it washed the back of her throat.

"Ahh," he groaned as the tension left his body.

Kenny slumped against the counter, trying to catch his breath. Dear Lord, she was gonna be the death of him. But oh, what a way to go, he thought. He smiled down at her as she moved up his body, a satisfied smile on her full lips.

"Does that mean you've changed your mind about hooky nooky day?"

*****

Connie couldn't believe she'd just blown Kenny off in his kitchen. But he'd looked so damn hot standing there in his freshly pressed dress shirt and silk tie, coffee cup in hand. She had gotten hotter by the minute. Nothing had mattered more in that moment than to have him cum in her mouth. Embarrassment over her actions threatened to make her turn her gaze away from his, but she refused. Though it was still new to her, this man obviously found something about her he liked and had spent last night proving to her that every part of her was okay by him.

"You didn't answer my question," he said, reaching down to pull up his pants and refasten them.

She reached for his coffee cup and took a sip. Connie wondered briefly if he would drink from it again. After all, she had just swallowed his cum. She recognized she was looking for some flaw that would make him seem more real. More like your typical everyday guy and not the perfect being he appeared to be. She needed something to make him seem obtainable. Someone within her reach. Connie hated that even after last night she still had doubts about what he wanted from her and what role he wanted her to play in his life.

"No hooky nooky day," she said, laughing at the hopeful expression on his face.

Kenny reached for his coffee cup and took a swallow before leaning over to kiss her on the lips. When his tongue did a sweep of her mouth, her already wet panties dampened further.

"Okay," he said, running his hand between her legs and making contact with her wet panties.

"You're gonna be late," she whispered.

Her breath left her as his fingers moved around the side of her panties to stroke her wet flesh.

"Yeah," he said, gazing intently into her eyes.

His finger pushed into her hot and sensitive flesh, and she grabbed his shoulders to keep from falling.

"I just wanted a taste before I left for work. This gives you something to look forward to all day. And it gives me a reason to shuffle some stuff around and get off early," he said with a final stroke against her swollen nub.

She watched mesmerized as he brought his finger to his nose. He closed his eyes and inhaled deeply of her smell.

"There's nothing better than the smell of you aroused," he said before licking his finger. "Well, maybe the taste of that arousal."

Her stomach clenched at the sight of him licking his finger.

"Give me strength," she said under her breath.

"Hmm, give us both strength," he said, kissing her deeply again. "Hey, I have to go."

"Oh, right," she said, trying to gather her senses. "Just let me run back upstairs and get my bag real quick."

"I said I have to leave not you," he said, reaching for his keys on the counter.

"Here. Just lock up when you're done or you can stay and be here when I get home, your choice. I took the liberty of writing down the code to the alarm. I put it on the fridge for you," he said, leaning down to plant another quick kiss on her parted lips, and then he was gone.

First, she just stood there staring at the key in her hand before cautiously glancing around. She was all alone in Kenny's house. She couldn't believe it. Connie pinched herself to make sure she wasn't dreaming before twirling around in a circle. Maybe just maybe he was for real.

Chapter 19

Connie hummed a little tune to herself as she headed upstairs to get her overnight bag. She checked her watch. It was almost two o'clock. Kenny had mentioned possibly getting off work early, and she wanted to be there when he arrived, she thought with a mischievous glint in her eyes. She was almost at the top of the stairs when the doorbell rang.

"Connie, can you get that?" Tammy called from the kitchen.

"Yep," she yelled and bounced back down the stairs, her steps lighter than they had been in a long time.

She opened the door to find Brenda on the other side, a perturbed expression on her face. Dammit. Why had she forgotten her overnight bag earlier when she had left the house? Connie could kick herself because now here she was mentally preparing herself to deal with Brenda's obviously pissy attitude.

"Constance Eunice Banks, you have been avoiding me," she said, coming through the door and closing it behind her.

"Obviously not well enough," Connie mumbled under her breath before moving back towards the stairs.

"Constance," Brenda called.

Her foot had just landed on the first step. A slow breath left her lungs before she turned to see her sister standing there, hands on her hips.

"Yes, Brenda?"

Patience, she told herself. Just keep your cool and things will go smoothly. Listen to what she has to say, and then you can leave. The thought of being there when Kenny walked in brought a smile to her face. Already thoughts of how she would be waiting for him when he arrived home were taking root. Maybe she'd meet him naked at the door? Or in bed with nothing on but one of his silk ties. Heat crept up her body at the thought of his reaction.

"Don't yes Brenda me. I have been calling you since yesterday afternoon, and you have not returned one of my phone calls."

"I've been busy getting ready for finals."

"Uh huh and I'm supposed to believe you were up studying late last night. I was here until close to midnight, and you weren't home yet."

"I was at a private tutoring session," she mumbled.

It wasn't exactly a lie. All the lessons she'd learned last night under Kenny's masterful tutelage would definitely come in handy.

"Is that your sly way of telling me you were having sex with Kenny last night?"

Sometimes saying nothing was the best thing when dealing with Brenda. So she continued standing there simply staring down at where her sister stood with her best blank look on her face.

"So you have slept with him."

It was more of a statement than a question, so Connie didn't feel compelled to answer. A look of disapproval crossed her face. She didn't know if it was because she'd managed the act without her or because she'd slept with him in general. But either way, the look was irritating the hell out of her.

"And if I have, it would be your business because? You've never questioned who I've slept with in the past."

She tried to put a lid on her growing anger. Arguing with her sister was not how she had wanted to spend her afternoon. It would only succeed in putting her in a bad mood for when she saw Kenny, and she didn't want to waste any of her time with him thinking about Brenda.

"I thought the idea was to keep him around for a little while, not just fuck him and let him go on his way."

"And how do you know he's going on his way?"

Though her sister's words irritated her to no end, Connie realized she couldn't be but so upset because hadn't those same thoughts wandered through her head a time or two today as well? What if now that they had slept together, he would make up some excuse to end things? She wished Brenda would get the hell out of her head.

"Well, maybe not yet. But you had better bet it is coming. He's gotten what he wants, Constance. Why would he stick around now?"

Brenda's tone asked how she could be so stupid as to think he'd stick around just to be with her. Weren't those the same thoughts that had been trying to bring her down off her high all day? She had managed to push them back with thoughts of how tenderly he had held her. How softly he'd spoken words of endearment in her ear as she had come down off of a particularly strong orgasm. How he had given her the key to his damn house for goodness sake. Those could not be the actions of a man who only wanted to get in her pants and leave.

"Oh my god, that is what you think isn't it? You actually think something more than sex can come of this little thing you and he have going on."

The look of utter disbelief on Brenda's face pushed a button deep inside of her. The look said she was playing the fool once again for a man.

"Con, who was at the door," Tammy asked, coming into the foyer. "Oh," she said, her expression saying it all as she looked at Brenda.

"Don't start with me," Brenda said, crossing her arms over her chest. "As a matter of fact, I have a bone to pick with you and those other so called best friends of my sister."

"Oh. Well, I'm sure everyone would like nothing better than to hear what you have to say to us. How about you come back when we are all here together? I'll give you a call to schedule something," Tammy replied, sarcasm lacing her words.

"No, how about I just start with you and work my way through the rest when I see them. How could you have allowed my sister, your supposed best friend, to sleep with that man? My god, she's barely known him a week."

The look of shock on Tammy's face was comical. Her mouth opened in a perfect circle, and she clasped her hands over her mouth before she began squealing.

"You slept with him," she asked in a stage whisper.

Though just as melodramatic as Brenda's face had been moments ago, Connie couldn't keep the smile off her face at the look on Tammy's. All she could do was nod.

"Do the other girls know?" she asked, still whispering.

Connie shook her head.

"You told Brenda first?" she asked, disbelief replacing her shock and a frown puckering her brows.

The look Connie gave her answered her question without words.

"Oh, she guessed, huh?"

Connie nodded.

"Hello," Brenda yelled. "I asked you a question. This is not something to be happy about. Don't you realize now that he's satisfied, his apparent curiosity he will move on?"

Connie gave a deep sigh of frustration. There were days when she had to wonder why she'd been blessed, and she used the word loosely, with a sister like Brenda. She'd long ago given up any delusions of them having a close relationship or even being friends for that matter. For years, she had sat by and idly listened to all of her disparaging remarks about how she looked, how she dressed, what she ate and the list went on. She was sick and tired of Brenda always trying to burst her bubble. She had finally met a guy who didn't seem to care that her sister was the "pretty one" and she was just the "cute one". Kenny didn't seem to care that her thighs were flabby. He didn't care that her breasts were too heavy to ever be perky. And it didn't seem to bother him in the least that she didn't have tons of experience with other men. He liked her the way she was, faults and all. But for how long? The thought came unwanted across her mind, but she refused to think in those terms right now and pushed it away.

"Look, Brenda, you don't know Kenny. He's not like that," she said, trying to convince herself as much as her sister.

Brenda gave a snort of laughter.

"Yeah and you say that based on what experience? Because he said a few kind words after you two had sex? Because he held you close before he kicked you out of his house last night? Or did he allow you to stay over for a morning fuck? Grow up, Constance. Men are after only one thing, and if we women give it up too easily, then we can't expect a man to stay around for long. So you can kiss your pretty boy goodbye now that he's had his taste," she said, her lip curling in apparent anger.

Connie just looked at her sister. She was in no mood to hear any more of what she had to say, and she had the option to leave. She thought of the key to Kenny's house and her destination before she'd answered the door.

"Look, Brenda, thanks for your concern or whatever it is," she began before the doorbell chimed again. "Can you get that on your way out?" she asked, turning to head back upstairs for her overnight bag.

A gasp sounded from behind her. She turned around to see what was wrong now. The smile that broke out on her face was nothing short of smug as she glanced at her sister's shocked face.

"You were saying, Brenda," Tammy said, her eyebrows raised in question.

Connie walked back down the stairs to greet Kenny as he closed the door behind him. His eyes seemed to shine brighter when she stopped in front of him.

"Hey, what are you doing off so early," she asked, glancing at her watch uncertain of what she should do next.

Was she supposed to hug him? Give him a kiss hello? The decision was taken out of her hands when he pulled her to him for a hug before leaning down to kiss her softly on her shocked lips.

"I told you this morning I was going to try and shuffle some things around so we could spend some time together before you went to work," he said, gazing down into her eyes.

His gaze shifted from hers briefly, and it was as if for the first time he realized they weren't alone.

"Oh, sorry. Hey, Tammy. Brenda."

"Oh, don't apologize. I think it's great the only person you noticed when you came in was Connie," Tammy said, regarding Brenda with a tilt of her head.

"I'm out of here."

And just like that Brenda was gone with a slam of the door behind her.

"Was it something I said?" Kenny asked, a small smile on his face.

"Nope," Tammy said, winking at him before turning to leave them alone. "It was something you did. Tracy and Jamie are both gonna be mad they missed this one. Wait until I tell them."

Connie buried her face in Kenny's chest. God, it felt so good to have him hold her. Wrapped in his arms as she was now, the doubts quieted to mere whispers, which were easier to ignore. The doubts that had plagued her all afternoon disappeared behind a closed door.

"I get the feeling I missed something," he said, his warm breath against her ear.

She shivered in response.

"I'll tell you about it later," she said, moving out of his embrace. "I was just on my way to your house."

The smile he graced her with was so hot it caused her body to throb.

"You were, huh?"

"Yeah."

Kenny moved closer to her like a predator stalking its prey. She saw the look in his eyes, and a smile lifted her own lips. She began backing up the steps to her room.

"Connie, I'm gonna go out for a while," Tammy said, coming back into the foyer.

She glanced from Kenny to Connie and covered her mouth with her hands fighting back a laugh.

"I get the feeling you guys don't care. See ya," she said and left.

Connie looked at the closed door and then back at Kenny. The heat she felt moving through her body was mirrored in his gaze. They were home alone. She walked back down the stairs and grabbed his hands.

"Come on," she said, heading upstairs to her room.

"You know we can go to my place. It's only a few minutes away if that would be better. I think I can wait that long to get my hands on you," he said, following her down the hall to her room.

Pushing him into her room, Connie closed the door and made sure it was locked. She moved towards him and began undoing his tie. Making quick work of it, she tossed it over her shoulder, and then pulled his shirt tails free of his pants and unbuttoned them.

"Yeah, but those are minutes I don't want to spend in the car when I could spend them like this."

She pressed hot kisses across his bare chest to his hardened nipples and pulled one into her mouth. At his deep intake of breath, she began fondling the other until it was hard as the one between her lips.

"What if one of your roommates comes home and catches us?" He asked, his hands buried in her hair, holding her to his chest.

She looked up at him. Was he serious? All she could think about was getting her hands on his body as quickly as she could, and he was thinking of her roommates walking in on them.

"Don't be such a prude," she said, laughing up at him.

Disbelief clearly displayed in his eyes.

"A prude? I have never been called a prude in my life."

He pushed her back until she fell half hazard on the bed. Her legs spread slightly. Seeing him watching her, Connie spread her legs farther apart and moved her hand down between them. She ran her fingers against the crotch of her jeans.

"Prove it," she taunted.

It felt good to know she was the reason for the heat in his gaze. That she'd caused the bulge in his pants, which was threatening to burst free at any moment.

"Take off your jeans for me," he said, his voice coming out rough.

From her reclined position, she toed off her shoes first then unbuttoned her jeans and lifted her hips to push them down her legs. When they dangled around her calves Kenny pulled them the rest of the way off.

"Spread your legs."

The intensity of the gaze leveled at her caused heat to pool in the pit of her stomach. As if in a trance, she spread her legs wider as he had asked. When he began to rub his hand against the bulge in his pants all she could do was stare. She caught the corner of her lip between her teeth, her gaze locked on the hand caressing himself.

"I want you to touch yourself for me."

Her gaze shot to his, and heat of a different kind burned in her cheeks. Had he really just asked her to touch herself? The intensity in the hazel eyes staring back at her assured her she had heard correctly. She hesitated. Touching herself was something she had only done in the privacy of her own room. Late at night when the need to be fulfilled was too strong to be ignored.

"Touch yourself, Connie. I wanna watch you pleasure yourself," he said, his voice hoarse.

Taking a deep breath, she lifted her hips and removed her panties. She kicked them off in his general direction. His hand snagged them out of the air. Her eyes grew large as she watched him bring them to his nose and inhale. Without another thought, her hand moved between her legs and spread her cunt lips. She moved a finger to stroke against her throbbing clit.

"Oh," she breathed as she circled her finger around the nub feeling it get harder.

"That's it, sweetheart. Do you like how that feels."

"Yes," she whispered as moisture began to leak from between her spread legs into the crack of her ass.

Pleasure burned through her body, and her strokes increased in speed. Needing more, she shoved two fingers into her drenched opening. Through slanted eyes, she saw Kenny undo his slacks and push them down his powerful legs. He kicked them along with his shoes away from him, and he stood before her in just boxers, his dick pushed against the material. She watched as he stroked himself through the silky material, his gaze still focused on her fingers thrusting in and out. Connie realized there was something incredibly erotic about watching a man watch you pleasure yourself. The nervousness she had felt only moments ago took a back seat to the desire rushing through her.

"I love watching you play with yourself," he said, moving closer to the bed.

His gaze remained focused on the in and out motion of her fingers. When she pulled them out this time, she moved them around her swollen clit before sliding them back down between the lips of her cunt until she had them at her opening. She watched him closely as she inserted them inside. Her hips jerked forward as she entered to meet her thrusts. When she pulled them out she held them up for him to see. They were covered with her juices, and the smell of her arousal reached her nose. She inhaled deeply.

"You wanna taste?"

"I want more than a taste," he said, moving forward to wrap his lips around her fingers.

His tongue slipped between her digits and captured all the juices there. The warm suction of his lips caused her clit to throb painfully. Kenny's weight felt like heaven as he fell down upon her. His heated kisses burned her skin as he trailed those luscious lips of his down her neck into the deep v-neck of her shirt. His lower body rubbed against her heated flesh causing her clit to ache even more with need. He pushed her shirt up and over her head and stared down at her lace covered breasts.

"Beautiful," he breathed, taking in the sight of her heaving breasts.

A fresh wave of moisture gushed from Connie's heated center when his lips locked onto her puckered nipple through the material of her bra before he unhooked the front clasps and pushed the material apart.

"Absolutely beautiful," he said again.

Connie gasped her pleasure as he bit down on her hardened peak before pulling it into his mouth. She writhed against the knee that was now thrust between her open thighs.

"Kenny, please," she begged.

She wasn't sure what she was begging for exactly. For him to fill her or continue his assault on her breasts. Perhaps both.

Kenny raised his head, his eyes glazed over with desire.

"Please what? Tell me what you want, Connie," he said, moving to lie beside her, his leg still between her legs keeping them apart.

His hand moved from her heavy breasts across the swell of her stomach. He stopped once he reached her short pubic hairs. Connie thrust her hips upward hoping to let him know what she wanted.

"I sense you trying to tell me something, but I'm a little unclear on what it is you want."

Having had enough of his play, she grabbed his hand and placed it at her dripping outer lips.

"I want you to fuck me with your fingers," she gasped as she moved his fingers against her throbbing clit.

Kenny shoved two long fingers deep into her heated center. Her hips bucked off the bed to meet him. Those intrusive fingers thrust deeper, alternating his stroke between quick and slow and bringing her to a quick orgasm.

"Oh ... Oh," she panted, lifting her bare ass off the bed as wave after wave of pleasure moved through her.

He pulled his fingers from her heat and spread her juices around her swollen clit, and then he moved them beneath her nose. She caught a whiff of her scent on his fingers before he lifted his fingers to his mouth and licked them clean of her juices. A fresh wave of cum gushed from her. She would never get used to the sight or the thrill she got when she saw him tasting her.

"Mmm, tasty," he said, smiling down at her, his head supported in his open palm.

"Did that feel good, baby?" he asked, strong fingers moving against her swollen clit again. "I almost came with you. Just watching you fall apart makes me harder than I've ever been. Do you feel how hard you make me?"

He grabbed her hand and placed her palm on the bulge between his legs. She moved her hand against his groin, feeling him harden at her touch. When she heard a sigh of pleasure come from him, she applied more pressure.

"Oh yeah, baby, I like that," he whispered softly against her ear.

"I think you're wearing too many clothes," she said, leaning over to lightly brush her lips against his.

A soft chuckle sounded near her ear.

"Then let's do something about it."

He left her side to strip his boxers down and off. When he rejoined her on the bed, she felt his naked, heated flesh against her own.

"This was the longest day of my life. All I could think about was how much I wanted to see you writhing beneath me in out of control passion. I want to see you cum as I put my dick in your swollen cunt. Don't you want that? Don't you want me inside you?" Kenny asked as he leaned down and began suckling the nipple closest to him again.

Connie could barely form a thought, let alone an answer as he swirled his tongue around her sensitive peak.

"Oh, yes. Please, Kenny," she begged.

She closed her eyes, savoring the feel of the weight of his body against hers. At the moment, she didn't care whether or not Brenda was correct and Kenny would leave soon. All she cared about was the fact he was spreading her legs wide preparing to enter her. Sure, she realized she would have to wake up and face reality sooner or later. She just wasn't ready to do that just yet. Not just yet.

Chapter 20

"Oh god, it's only one o'clock," Connie said to the empty store as she struggled to stay awake.

She should have tried to get some sleep this evening while she'd been at Kenny's house. Yeah, right. All thoughts of sleep had fled her mind as soon as he had lain down beside her. He had snuggled close with his arm thrown across her waist. For long minutes, she had lain there, trying to think restful thoughts, but her body had been on a slow burn the moment he had touched her. When she had rolled over on her side, it had been to find his eyes wide open shining bright with desire, ready and willing to help her find alternate ways to spend the evening. Well, that's what she got because she was definitely paying for it now.

The bell over the door jangled to alert her someone had entered the store. She exhaled deeply and raised her head prepared to greet the customer, but the words died on her tongue as she saw two impeccably dressed white women enter the store. They wore designer labels, she was certain of it. They looked the type not to wear anything else. Their high heels clicked on the store floor as they walked the aisles. Sure, the neighborhood they lived in had some pretty wealthy people in it, but at this time of night or morning rarely did she see anything more than jeans and a t-shirt walking into the store.

"What are we doing in here again?" the redhead asked of her brunette friend.

"We're in here because I have the munchies like you would not believe, and I have nothing at home that will satisfy the craving."

The redhead gave her friend a bored expression.

"I told you not to take that hit, but you didn't listen."

Hit of what, Connie wondered. Then her eyes grew big as dawning came to her.

"Well, I only did it because Doug wanted me to. And he is so hot. No way I could have looked lame and not have done it," the brunette answered.

An unladylike grunt came from her redheaded friend as they continued their stroll of the aisles, having stopped at the chips.

"He wasn't that hot. It was the weed making you think he was. That shit was so strong it could make a monkey look appealing," she said, shaking her head. "Can you hurry up? I wanna get home so I can call Kenny."

Connie sat up from where she'd been leaning against the counter. Kenny. Had she said Kenny? She shook her head, laughing at herself. There were more guys in the world named Kenny than just hers. Hmmm. Her Kenny. She definitely liked the sound of that.

"Are you crazy? It's after one in the morning now. By the time I drop you off at home, it will be closer to two. Do you really think that's the best thing to do?"

"Yeah, well, he hasn't answered any of my other calls during the day. I figure I need to catch him off guard," she said, hunching her shoulders.

"Why did you dump him in the first place? You obviously didn't want him to leave?" the brunette asked shaking her head.

The redhead looked at her friend, a disbelieving look upon her face.

"Are you kidding me? He was always late."

Connie shook her head. Some men could be so inconsiderate. Kenny had only been late the one time. All other times he had surprised her showing up earlier than expected.

"Yeah, but he eventually got there, right? And he always made up for it didn't he?" the brunette asked her.

"Well, yeah, he made up for it the times he actually showed up. But near the end he just stopped making the effort to show up, and he was always working. I never came first with him. I don't even think I was a second or close third," the redhead continued whining.

Her friend turned to face her, a smile on her face.

"Aw, something you have in common," the brunette said, walking away from her friend.

"Okay, so I take my job very seriously. But when some of my clients come to me, they barely have time to breathe, and by the time they leave, they not only have time to breathe but to enjoy life. Can Kenny say the same about being an investment banker?"

Connie stood a little straighter. An investment banker. Her Kenny was an investment banker. Slow down, she told herself. There had to be more than one investment banker named Kenny in this city. She glanced around for the two women and located them by the freezer section.

"Oh, I don't know. I think it's pretty relaxing to sit back and have someone else make me tons of money," the brunette answered absently, opening the door of the freezer and peering inside.

"Okay," she said, handing the redhead some ice cream. "If he's always late and his job is more important than you are, why do you want him back so badly?"

"Duh, he was absolutely to die for hot. The connections I made when we did go out have put me in with a whole new type of client."

Connie had to put her hand over her mouth to keep them from hearing her laugh. She wondered what to die for hot looked like. An image of Kenny came quickly to mind.

The brunette's laughter flowed to the front of the store.

"But he won't even talk to you. It's obvious he's not interested in getting back with you any longer. I think you should let it go before you embarrass yourself further."

"I'm going to get him back. He's merely playing hard to get," the redhead said to her friend's back, a frown darkening her brow.

The brunette turned to her friend a patronizing smile on her face.

"Uh-huh. Keep telling yourself that, sweetheart, maybe it'll be true one day. I told you not to nag him so much. So what he was late a few times. Now he's not coming at all."

The brunette walked away from the redhead down another aisle. The redhead stood with her mouth open looking after her friend.

"But that shit was annoying as hell, Alexis. He needed to be taught a lesson," she said, rushing to catch up.

The woman, Connie now knew to be Alexis, turned to face the other woman.

"So tell me, Lori, how's the lesson going? Why don't you just face it? You threw away a perfectly good man," she said, turning away.

Alexis walked a few steps before turning back to Lori who was still standing in the same spot.

"Maybe he's found someone who isn't such a nagging bitch."

Lori's mouth opened in shock at her friend's comment. Connie was a little surprised herself. Somehow she hadn't expected people who dressed like they did to use such language.

"Nagging bitch? I'm not a nagging bitch. You're only saying that because you smoked that stuff. Wait until I remind you about this tomorrow," Lori said.

Alexis seemed to mull this over.

"You're probably right. Tomorrow I won't be nearly as honest with you. So you'd better pay attention tonight," Alexis said before turning to take another perusal of the candy aisle.

Connie leaned against the counter, a smile on her face. This was better than any keep you awake medicine on the market. These two could have a reality show. She would watch. They were funny. Especially Alexis.

"Oh, yeah," Lori said. "You just see who'll hold your hair back when you're puking your guts out."

Alexis turned to face Lori in the middle of the aisle.

"Look Lor, I'm your best friend in the whole wide world, and I love you to pieces. But you were wrong to dump Kenny, and we both know it. Now you want him back, and he's not having it. Just get over it and move on to someone else. Doug had a lot of cute friends at the party. What's wrong with one of them?"

When they headed towards the register, Connie straightened. Her smile was in place as Alexis dumped an armload of junk food down. She glanced from the junk food to Alexis and saw she was smiling at her.

"You know you have a really pretty face," Alexis said. "I should know I'm a modeling agent. It's my job to know these things."

Connie smiled at her and mumbled thank you under her breath. She began ringing up the items while Alexis and Lori continued their conversation.

"Now why can't you just find someone else? There are plenty of guys who'd jump at a chance to date you, and they'd probably be on time for at least one date out of the week."

Lori leaned a skinny hip against the counter and folded her arms across her chest. Connie glanced at her out of the corner of her eye and could have sworn she saw her bottom lip sticking out just a little. She even made pouting look pretty.

"Because I don't want anyone else. I want Kenneth Anderson Jamison dammit, and I will get him back."

Connie's hand paused over the bag of chips on the counter. Had she just said Kenneth Anderson Jamison? Maybe she was talking about another Kenneth Anderson Jamison. Her mind ran back over the conversation she'd just been eaves dropping in on. He was always late. Hadn't Kenny said he was running late to a date the night they'd met? Hadn't his girlfriend dumped him? The Kenny they were talking about was always working. As an investment banker. Oh god, her insides screamed. Connie was functioning on auto pilot as she finished ringing up the other items on the counter. Her mind was going over everything that had been said since they had entered the store. Lori wanted Kenny back. She was going to call him when she got home. How many other times had she called him? The night Kenny had met her at the library she'd called him, but he hadn't answered. How long would he continue to ignore her? The woman was gorgeous. And obviously quite determined.

"And what if said Kenneth Anderson Jamison doesn't want you?" Alexis asked, reaching in her teeny tiny purse and pulling out her credit card.

She handed it to Connie and tilted her head to the side and continued gazing at her.

"You ever thought of doing any modeling? You have great cheek bones."

Connie shook her head and took the card from her fingers. She hoped her own weren't trembling like her insides. This couldn't be happening. Of all the convenience stores for Kenny's ex-girlfriend to walk into she had to walk into hers. Wait, that was from a movie, wasn't it? It didn't matter. She tried not to stare at Lori as she waited for Alexis' credit card to clear, but she couldn't help it. She had realized the woman was beautiful when she had walked in the store, but now as she stood directly in front of her, Connie realized breathtaking was more apt of a description. This was what Kenny was used to dating.

Lori had long red hair that hung down her back. She had that perfect handful of breasts all men loved. At least, that's what the books all said. She had a barely there waist with hips that flared ever so slightly. Definitely not the birthing hips her grandma always said she had.

Connie pulled the receipt from the cash register and handed it to Alexis along with a pen.

"If you would sign on the line please," she mumbled.

What the hell was Kenny doing with her if this was what he was used to? Talk about slumming. A dull throbbing began at her temple. Alexis handed her back the slip and grabbed her bag of goodies. She pulled out a card from her purse.

"Give me a call if you ever consider doing any modeling. We have had great demand for full-figured models lately. I think you'd photograph well."

Connie took the card. Not really seeing it.

"Thank you," she said, watching them leave.

"And thank you for making me face reality sooner than later," she whispered to the now empty store.

Chapter 21

Connie sat outside Kenny's house, early Saturday morning, debating whether or not she should go inside. The key he had given her just yesterday was burning a hole in her pocket. She could almost hear it taunting her with what she wanted versus what she knew was best for her own peace of mind.

When leaving his house last night, she'd had every intention of returning this morning when she got off. Thoughts of how they'd spent the afternoon had followed her to work, but then she'd seen firsthand the type of woman he was used to. Knowing you didn't fit the bill and having it smack you in the face were two entirely different things.

Memories of Lori's small perfect body had continued to haunt her for hours after she'd left the store. Thoughts of how he could have ever touched her own imperfect form tumbled over and over in her head. No matter how many times she had reminded herself he had not only touched it but had tasted every inch of her failed to give her the comfort and security she needed.

Connie ran shaky fingers through her hair and placed her head against her steering wheel. The headache that had begun when she'd realized the very perfect redhead was Kenny's ex-girlfriend was now pounding a relentless beat against her temple. She had gone into this believing it a temporary thing. Then Kenny had done the unexpected, he had asked for her to give what they had a chance, and she had done the unimaginable. She had begun to believe it could be real. But last night she'd been faced with reality. She was on borrowed time with Kenny until he came to his senses and realized there were hundreds of thousands of women better suited for him than she was.

"I am so far in over my head," she said. "What am I going to do?"

Ring … ring….

She jumped up in her seat and hit her head on the roof of her car.

"Dammit," she yelled, rubbing the top of her head.

She grabbed her cell phone from where it lay on the passenger seat beside her. A quick check of the caller id confirmed what she already suspected. A deep sigh moved through her body. Now or later it all added up to the same thing.

"Hello."

"I was just wondering if you were planning on sitting outside in your car all morning."

The cheerful tone of Kenny's voice on any other day would have brought a smile to her face. Today it only succeeded in adding to her misery. Had he spoken with Lori last night while she had been at work? Was that why he was so happy this morning? Were they in the process of working things out? Or worse had she been over. Turning her gaze towards the house, she saw his silhouette in the upstairs window. She wondered if that was his bedroom window. The thought brought unwanted memories of their time spent together in that room and the many things they'd done. Moisture pooled between her legs as her thoughts lingered on their time together. Never had anyone taken the time with her as Kenny had. He'd allowed her to not only explore his body, but he'd allowed her to discover what turned her on. She was going to miss that.

"Hey, you still there or did you fall asleep on me?"

His soft laughter filtered across the phone lines and caressed her skin.

"Uh, no. Sorry about that. I'm just really tired this morning," she said, hoping he wouldn't hear the strain in her voice.

"Well, there's a nice soft bed waiting for you inside. But first you have to get out of the car, sweetheart."

He'd called her that on several other occasions, but this morning it sounded especially sweet to her ears. Tears welled up at the back of her eyes. Would anyone else ever call her sweetheart? If they did, could it possibly sound as sweet as when he said it? A wave of loneliness came over Connie as she sat in her car, her head against her seat rest. In such a short period of time, he had come into her life and given her hope that maybe things would be different this time. A tear slid down her cheek, and she didn't bother to wipe it away. It would only be replaced by the many she was holding at bay with sheer willpower.

"I'm sorry, Kenny," she said softly into the phone.

Connie felt as if she needed to apologize for not having enough faith in him. In her opinion, he had done everything he could to dispel her earlier thoughts of him. Kenny had set himself apart from all the other guys she'd had the misfortune of knowing. But as hard as she'd tried, Connie had never been completely able to accept what he had seemed to be offering, a chance to live her dream. Thoughts of how long before he woke up and realized he could do better were always at the back of her mind.

"Sorry for what, Connie?"

She could hear the confusion in his voice. It was mixed with something else she couldn't quite decipher.

"I'm sorry that I'm not stronger," she said, shaking her head.

Another tear slipped down her cheek. She never should have gone out on that first date with him. She should have stuck to her guns and continued to say no. That way she never would have known what she could never truly have. A deep sigh came across the phone line, and Connie cringed.

"Why don't you come inside so we can talk about it? I have coffee made, and I can fix you some breakfast," he said, his voice soft and coaxing.

The urge to give in and do as he asked was so strong her heart constricted. What lay in store for her inside that house was too good to be true? Accepting would only delay the inevitable. The day when he would wake up beside her and see her the way others had seen her in the past. That would be the day he realized he had picked the wrong sister. The day he'd call Lori up and see if they could work it out. Connie didn't want to be around for that day.

"I can't," she answered finally. "I think it's best if I go home. Maybe after I get some sleep, I'll come back over and we can talk then."

It was a lie, and he probably knew it as well as she did. She had no intentions of ever crossing his doorstep again. And once he got over being dumped twice within one week, he would realize she was doing them both a favor.

"Why not just stay now since you're outside? You said it yourself. You're tired and need to get some rest. I can run you a hot bath, and then you can get some sleep. I brought some work home with me, so I won't disturb you."

He was being so considerate and thoughtful. Hot tears rolled freely down her cheeks.

"Kenny, this past week has been the best week of my life. I have enjoyed being with you so much, but I think it's time we both stopped kidding ourselves. I mean how long can this really last between us? How long before you realize you no longer find me intriguing and start looking for a way to let me down easy?"

"But how do you know that, Connie?" he asked, his voice coming out raw and full of emotion. "You have condemned it already. Why not at least see how far it can go before you pass sentence? It might surprise you in the end."

No, she wanted to scream. It would only make it worse. She'd have way too much time to fall more in love with him than she already was. Connie's mouth opened in shock as dawning came with the rising of the sun. As the last remnants of night gave way to the bright sunshine of a new day, she finally admitted to herself what she'd been fighting all week. She was in love with Kenny Jamison. She ran her fingers through her hair and wondered how the hell that had happened. They'd only known each other a week.

"We would only be delaying the inevitable. I'd rather just say my goodbyes now."

"And if I don't want to say goodbye, Constance? What if I don't want to give you up? What if I told you that you have already taken over a large part of my heart?"

"It's not about what you want, Kenny. It's about what's best for me," Connie said, trying not to completely break down.

It was getting considerably harder to speak around the tight wad of pain that had lodged itself in her throat.

"I think what's best for you is me and vice versa," he said softly.

She didn't detect the first hint of arrogance in his tone. How should she respond to that? Tell him you agree, her heart screamed. Tell him you had a momentary melt down but you're fine now. Then get out of the car and run to him as fast as you can. But she couldn't do that. Kenny owned her heart. She didn't dare think how bad it would be if she stayed and then later he left. She refused to acknowledge the silent pleading of her heart to reconsider. And her heart's silent question of what if he didn't leave. What if Kenny was truly different?

"I don't."

The lie barely made it past the knot in her throat.

"I don't believe you. What happened between last night and this morning? When you left last night, you were coming back this morning, and I don't mean just to sit outside my house in your car. What happened?"

His voice was no longer soft and coaxing. Frustration and anger now rang clear and who could blame him. When she had left his house, it had been with a promise of coming back this morning to awaken him in the sweetest manner possible. This was not the wakeup call either of them had planned, but she realized it was the one she'd been running from all week.

"I stopped listening to my body and started listening to my brain."

"Yeah, well, tell your brain for me to shut the hell up. Maybe you need to start listening to your heart, Connie? What does your heart tell you to do?"

Connie leaned her head against her headrest and listened to her heart. It was screaming at her to get out of the car and go inside to the man she loved.

"My heart doesn't get a vote in this matter," she finally said.

The pain in her chest intensified as her heart broke a little more. They said what didn't kill you made you stronger. After this, providing she didn't have to be committed to an insane asylum, she should be as strong as Wonder Woman.

"Constance Banks, either you come in this house right now or I will come outside and get you," he threatened.

Sounds of movement came across the phone line. She looked at the house towards the upstairs window he had been standing in and no longer saw his outline.

"I'm going home, Kenny. I'll call you later and maybe we can talk about this further. But not now," she said and hung up.

Tears streamed down her face as she pulled away from the curb. She didn't bother to try and brush them aside. What would be the point? They'd only bring fresh ones in their place.

A few minutes later she sat outside her home. She spent a few minutes behind the wheel trying to get herself together. She wiped the tears from her eyes and prayed she could hold off any more until she got to the privacy of her room. She glanced at her watch and breathed a small sigh of relief. At least it was too early for her roommates to be up and about yet. So she wouldn't have to explain why she was at home or why she had been crying.

Connie opened the door slowly. She breathed a small sigh of relief as the quiet of the house surrounded her. Her hand was still on the door handle when she realized she wasn't alone in the foyer. Turning slowly around, she found three pairs of eyes staring at her. Tammy and Tracy were sitting on the steps and Jamie was leaning against the wall adjacent to the door. What the hell were they all doing up? She took a shaky breath and tried to pull herself together enough to speak.

"Good morning. What are you guys doing up?" she asked, heading for the stairs and her escape, but her two roommates on the steps blocked her way.

"What are you doing home? I thought you'd be at Kenny's after work this morning," Tammy asked, eying her closely.

Connie didn't like the feeling of dread coming over her. Why were they all up waiting on her?

"I decided to come home and get some rest first. You know how wild I sleep when I'm tired. And I didn't get much rest yesterday before I went into work," she said, pushing thoughts of her afternoon spent in Kenny's arms to the back of her mind.

"I guess I'll see you guys in a few hours."

She stood waiting for Tammy and Tracy to move so she could get to the safety of her bedroom when the doorbell chimed. Connie glanced from the closed door to her roommates who hadn't budged.

"Since you're closer, why don't you answer that?" Tracy said from her seat on the steps, her arms folded over her small chest.

For the first time in her life, she prayed for it to be Brenda.

"I'd just like to get upstairs to my room. Please," she said, pleading with them with her eyes to allow her to escape while she could.

"Just remember we love you," Jamie said, moving to the door and opening it.

Her eyes grew large at the sight of a very pissed off Kenny standing in the doorway. He had on a t-shirt and jeans; on his feet were flip flops. His unshaven jaw lent an air of danger to his already stunning good looks. His eyes were bright with anger as he took in the sight of her. She should run to her room. It would be easy. She could just barrel right through Tammy and Tracy who were now standing up on the steps. But she couldn't move under the intensity of his glare. Connie felt like a trapped rabbit.

"Good morning, Kenny," Jamie said, closing the door once he'd entered. "I think you two have something to discuss, so we'll just go back to bed."

Wait, these were her friends. They were supposed to be on her side. They weren't supposed to be leaving her to face him alone. Connie watched in disbelief as her friends headed back to their rooms.

"Where are you guys going?" she asked them.

"Back to bed," Tammy said, giving her a small smile before she followed Jamie up the steps.

Tracy turned back towards her.

"If I were you, Con, I'd listen to what he has to say. He looks pretty pissed off," she said, throwing her a sympathetic look over her shoulder as she climbed the rest of the stairs.

"No kidding," she said under her breath turning to face Kenny.

Connie hesitated before lifting her gaze to meet his. She felt her stomach bottom out. His eyes clearly reflected his anger. But was he angry because he'd had to leave the comfort of his home so early in the morning? Or was it because yet another woman had dumped him before he'd gotten the chance? Whatever the reason he wasn't happy.

Chapter 22

Kenny tried to get his anger under control as he stared at Connie who hadn't moved from her position by the stairs. The short distance from his home to hers hadn't given his temper enough time to cool. He felt it clawing at his insides. He had been prepared to lay his soul on the line for her this morning and she had run. He tried to remind himself that he had been struggling with doubts and confusion over their relationship for most of the night. His heart fighting for what it knew to be true. At four o'clock this morning, he had finally admitted to the empty room that he loved Connie. Saying it out loud had somehow made it more real to him. He'd shouted it over and over several times until it seemed to echo in the emptiness of his home. A home he hoped wouldn't remain empty for long.

The thought had thrilled him when he'd first stumbled across it during the wee hours of the morning. A huge smile had split his face as he'd been up pacing, contemplating what it meant. Then he'd stopped midstride as panic began to set in. What did he know about love? He who had dated a woman who annoyed the hell out of him for four months simply because she looked good on his arm. How did he even know what he was feeling was real? What if it was as his mother had suggested? Just a deep case of lust. And then the dreaded, what if she didn't feel the same way about him? That thought had almost brought on an anxiety attack. Could it be possible the feelings were only one sided? His ego had answered with a resounding – no way, followed by an arrogant - how could she not be just as much in love with him as he was with her? But for the first time he paid it no attention because stranger things had happened. Like the fact he found himself in love with a woman who a few short weeks ago he wouldn't have looked at twice.

Plopping down on the side of the bed with his head in his hands, all of Kenny's past failed relationships had come to the forefront. Relationships that had been based on a mutual need, and when that need was fulfilled, it was over. What did he know about a real relationship that involved the constant give and take he'd witnessed over the years with his parents? What if he did something to mess it up? His chest had hurt at the thought of his causing Connie pain in any way. But then it came to him. The thing that set this apart from any other relationship he had ever had in the past. He wanted her in his life and he was prepared to do whatever he had to do to keep her by his side.

Kenny took a deep breath and brought himself back to the present and the situation at hand. Uncertainty flashed in the depths of Connie's eyes. And was that even just a little fear? She should be afraid. Afraid he didn't throw her over his shoulder and drag her upstairs to her bed. Even his anger couldn't keep his feelings of need at bay. Even now as he stood watching her, he wanted her and not just to sate his body. He needed her to fill all the empty holes in his soul. Holes he hadn't known were there until he'd met her.

"Do you think you're the only one who's afraid, Connie?" he asked finally.

Staring at her now, he could see the tear streaks on her cheeks and the shimmer of tears in her eyes as she continued to gaze warily at him. A part of him just wanted to take her in his arms and assure her he wouldn't hurt her. That he loved her too much. But he couldn't. Not yet. Damn, he was tired all of a sudden. He hadn't gotten much sleep last night and had looked forward to holding Connie in his arms as they slept the morning away. A deep sigh moved through him as he wondered if that would happen anytime soon.

"Well, you're not," he said, pushing away from the door.

He moved to sit on the steps at her feet, his head lowered in his hands.

"When I first met you… It's hard to believe it's only been a week. But you stood behind that counter and you weren't impressed with anything about me. Man, you did some pretty healthy damage to my ego," he said, laughing softly as he recalled that night.

"You made me curious to discover who this woman was who could resist the famous Kenny Jamison charm. When I actually looked at you, my disbelief and confusion grew. You were nothing like the women I normally found myself attracted to. But there I was barely able to contain the hard on I was getting by looking at you."

Kenny saw shock register in her eyes.

"I wasn't immune to your charm, Kenny. I'd have to be dead not to notice you. I was just determined not to give you the reaction you were used to receiving from women. Besides you were there to get gas, and then you would be gone."

Connie moved to sit down on the steps a couple up from him.

"We see how far I've gone, don't we?"

He laughed.

"Yeah, but the jury's still out on how long you would have stayed," she said, not looking at him.

So now we finally get to the root of the problem, Kenny thought.

"Look, Connie, I admit when I asked you out that first night, it was only because I was curious about you and your effect on me. But it didn't take me long to realize one night wasn't enough. I liked the feeling of excitement I got when I was going to see you. I've even come to enjoy the butterflies I get when I get my first look at you. And I love the hard on I get every time you touch me," he said, turning on the steps to look up at her. "I guess what I'm saying is if you think you're in this by yourself, then you couldn't be more wrong. My feelings have never been more invested in a relationship. I might have asked you out for the wrong reasons, but I'm staying for all the right ones."

It was not quite the declaration of love he had planned for last night, but this was not the time or place to declare his undying love for her. He watched her sitting there, wringing her hands in her lap. Inside he pleaded with her to make the right decision. To put them both out of their misery. When she lifted her gaze to meet his, Kenny felt his heart drop to his feet. Misery was reflected in her eyes, and it tore at his insides. Maybe he should just leave now. Make it easier for her. He dropped his gaze. Hmph, who was he kidding? It would make it easier on them both. He wasn't going to like what she was about to say, and he knew it.

"Kenny, when I'm with you, I forget about everything else. I forget I'm about forty pounds overweight. And that I'm not the best dresser. I forget about a past that has proven time and time again how a girl like me can never get a guy like you."

He lifted his head. Maybe he'd been wrong about what he'd seen in her eyes. Hope soared in his soul.

"But last night I came face to face with a reality I couldn't ignore."

His heart plummeted when he saw tears begin to stream down her cheeks. She was no longer looking at him.

"Knowing that I'm not as pretty or as thin as the type of woman you're used to is one thing, but actually seeing it in the flesh is something completely different. All those old doubts and feelings of inadequacy came crashing in on me. And the one question I can't seem to escape. How long before you realize you can do better than me?"

Not for the first time he wondered who could have done this to such a beautiful woman. Who could have intentionally taken her feelings and cast them away only to leave these insecurities and doubts of her beauty. He moved to the step where Connie sat and pulled her into his arms. His heart ached for the obvious pain she'd experienced at the hands of others and their callous treatment of her heart.

"Connie, I hate that you've been hurt so badly in the past. I wish I could do something to take it all away. But I can't. All I can do is show you how good it can be for us. All I'm asking is for you to have faith in what we could have."

"For you to have faith in me," he added silently.

"Kenny, I don't know if I can," she answered. "Everything I've ever known has told me you and I can't work."

Kenny felt her arms move around his waist to hold him closer to her body.

"I don't know about you, but I make my own decisions about who I want to be with. And if you want to be with me, Connie, then you will have to take that big leap of faith. I promise I will be there to catch you."

With one last squeeze, a gentle kiss placed on her soft lips, Kenny released her and got up from the steps.

"The decision is yours, Connie. What do you say?" he asked, holding his hand out for her to take it.

With all his heart Kenny wanted her to reach out for him. The last slivers of his ego refused to allow him to beg her further. He'd already come after her when she'd run.

She had to make this decision on her own. Either she wanted him enough to take a chance on forging a new path or she didn't.

When tear filled eyes lifted to his, he knew he had his answer. He allowed his hand to drop to his side and moved towards the door. She'd been through a lot in her past, and he could accept that she wasn't ready yet. He didn't know if she would ever be ready, but he had to believe she would be. He'd gone through a lot of women to find her, and he wouldn't let her go now.

He turned back to her, his hand on the knob.

"Don't think this is over. I'm used to getting what I want. And let there be no doubt that what I want is you in my bed and by my side."

Kenny gave her one of his sexiest smiles before opening the door and closing it softly behind him. He stood on the small porch listening to the soft sobs from the other side. He could still see her sitting there, misery clearly written on her face and tears streaming down her cheeks. He longed to go back inside and hold her tight, promising everything would be alright. But he couldn't. She'd made her decision, and he would allow her to stew in it for a while.

He reluctantly left and headed for his car. His steps were surprisingly light for a guy who for all intents and purposes had been dumped for the second time in as many weeks. But not for long. He'd seen the longing in Connie's eyes when she'd looked at him. He'd give her a reprieve for today because he loved her. But after that all bets were off. It would be a full on attack because he loved her. He'd always wanted to play the role of knight in shining armor. He just never guessed his damsel in distress would need saving from herself.

Chapter 23

Connie hated to go downstairs, but she couldn't continue to hide out in her room forever. Besides she had to work tonight. She'd agreed to come in a little earlier, so the guy on duty, Paul, could leave. It wasn't like she had anything else to do on a Saturday night.

She pushed herself up from the side of the bed where she'd been sitting staring off into nothing for the past thirty minutes. Doubts over her decision weighed heavy on her tense shoulders. Had she done the right thing? Could she and Kenny have worked out had she just given them a chance? They'd done okay for the week they'd been together.

"Oh, well. What's done is done now. After this morning I won't have to worry about it," she said to the empty room.

It was how her life was going to be now that she'd kicked him out of it. She didn't want anyone else. She couldn't begin to think anyone would ever be able to take his place.

Connie left her room moving slowly down the steps. At the bottom she saw her friends getting ready to go out. Great. She should have waited just a little longer before coming down.

"Hey, Con. You okay?" Tracy asked, concern in her voice and on her face.

"Yep," she answered simply, moving to get a jacket from the coat closet.

The store had a tendency to be a little chilly overnight.

"You wouldn't be lying to us would you," Jamie questioned, a look of disbelief in her eyes.

"Nope," she replied.

"You got anything more than one word answers?" Tracy asked, leaning against the door looking at her.

Connie thought on this for a moment and shook her head. She didn't feel like talking. They were lucky they got anything at all.

"Look, Con, we don't know exactly what happened between you and Kenny, but by all accounts, it doesn't look like we need to go kick his ass. Are we right on that?" Tammy asked.

Misery over her own actions threatened to bring on another onslaught of tears. With a lowered head, all she could manage was a small nod of acknowledgement. No, the fault of this all fell on her already slumped shoulders.

"So what you're telling us is that it was you? You let an absolutely great guy, from the little we know about him, just walk out of your life?" Jamie asked.

That was almost laughable. No, she hadn't just let him walk out of her life. She'd kicked him out. The tears she thought had stopped came back to clog her throat. So she merely nodded. Her heart ached anew, and all she wanted to do was go back upstairs and crawl in bed.

"Why, Connie? He seemed to really like you," Jamie questioned, confusion was written all over her face.

"I don't wanna talk about it," she managed.

She struggled to hold back the tears. Couldn't they understand? Didn't they know? It wasn't as if they hadn't been right there with her when all of her other "walks on the other side" had backfired. She shouldn't have to explain this to them.

"Don't you think you deserve to have somebody special in your life?" Tammy asked.

"I don't wanna talk about it," she repeated.

She closed the closet door with a slam. Shock registered on her friends faces.

"Look, guys, let's go. Connie will talk to us when she's ready," Tracy said, looking at her closely.

"I gotta get to work. I'll see you guys in the morning."

That said, she quickly left the house. In the car, she allowed the tears she'd been holding back to fall freely. This was going to be another great night. Last night she had talked herself out of a relationship with the man she loved. What would tonight hold?

Once outside the store, Connie checked her reflection in her visor mirror. Her eyes were puffy, and her nose was running. Misery dimmed her normally bright brown eyes. In short, she looked how she felt. Like hell. Oh, well. There was nothing she could do about it now. She was already here, and there was no way she was going to go back home in the off chance of running into her roommates again. She checked her watch and saw it was barely eight o'clock. She was a little earlier than agreed, but Paul would appreciate that. Besides she had nothing else to do. That was going to be the story of her life. Connie wondered if Roger needed help on the day shift. Once school was out, she'd need something to occupy her time. Still thinking on this, she got out of the car and entered the store. She waved to the guy on duty.

"Hey, Paul. You wanna head on out since I'm here?" she asked.

She knew he and his wife had plans for the evening.

"You're a doll, Connie," he said, grabbing his stuff from behind the counter and going to the back to clock out.

"I'll see you next weekend," he said on his way out.

"Yep, see ya," she said and took the seat behind her.

She pulled her back pack onto the counter, glad she'd left it in the car this morning when she'd come in. She may as well see if she could get some studying done. Maybe instead of working for the summer at the gas station, she could take some summer courses. That would put her ahead for next year. It bore more thought. Connie made a note to call her parents to get their thoughts on it. Or maybe she'd go visit them for a month or so. A change of scenery and all.

"Okay, who shall it be first? Physics or Women's Studies?" she asked, looking from one book to the other.

An hour later, after reading the same passage four times, Connie closed her book with a snap and ran her fingers through her loose hair. She couldn't concentrate. Thoughts of her time spent with Kenny kept clouding her mind. She pulled her hair up into a high ponytail and secured it there. She wondered what he was doing right now. Humph, she grunted. He's probably out with someone as equally as hot as he is and forgetting all about you.

"That's right, Connie, let's think happy thoughts," she mumbled to herself.

The loud sounds of motorcycles outside the store pulled her attention from the path of misery it was heading towards. She sat transfixed as a group of five on bikes, all in different colors, pulled into the gas station. She stood up so she could get a better view of them. Connie's eyes grew huge as one of the bikers riding a black and silver bike got off with one smooth motion. Though he had his helmet on, she knew instantly it was Kenny. There was no one else who could fill out a black leather jacket the way he did. As he sauntered towards the other leather clad bikers, her mouth watered at the sight of him. She was certain there was no one who moved with as much confidence as he did. Suddenly panic took hold of her. She turned away from the window. Oh, god, what if he came into the store. She was in no frame of mind to see him just yet. She was still an emotional wreck and feared she might say something completely stupid or worse yet jump him at first sight. Glancing back out the store window, Connie saw him take off his helmet, a smile on his face. Her breath caught in her chest at the sight of him. He was gorgeous, and he'd been hers.

As she watched Kenny and his friends laughing and joking, she could imagine the sparkle in his eyes. A frown puckered her brow as she saw him almost double over in amusement. Well, it was nice to see he wasn't suffering as much as she was over their break up. She turned away. It had been as she'd thought. He was having no trouble getting over her.

Not able to help herself, only moments passed before she turned back to get another look at him. Oh, god, he was coming into the store. His long legs ate up the short distance from the pumps to the door. What was she going to do now? Any minute she would have to face him. *Okay, you can do this*, she told herself. Besides it wasn't like she had a choice in the matter. Connie braced herself for the sight of him up close, but when he came through the door, she felt tears sting the backs of her eyes. *This is what you gave up*, her heart screamed. *You are a fool, Constance Banks. A damned fool.*

Kenny paused when he came in the door and saw her standing behind the counter.

"Hey, Connie. You're in a little early aren't you," he said, his deep voice soothing her frayed nerves.

"Yeah," she answered simply.

She tried not to stare, but she couldn't help it. Though it had only been a few short hours since she'd seen him it felt like an eternity.

"Did you get any rest today? You look a little tired still."

The heat of his gaze roamed over her face not missing anything. Remember to breathe, she told herself. Just keep breathing.

"A little," she managed pass her dry throat.

Kenny's eyes continued to take in everything about her appearance causing Connie's body to come to life. The heat in his gaze felt like a physical caress. Her nipples hardened against the confines of her bra. She shifted uncomfortably under his close scrutiny.

"Did you need to get gas?" she asked.

A soft smile appeared across his face.

"Yep, and I came prepared with cash this time," he said, holding it out to her.

Connie couldn't keep her own smile at bay as she recalled their first meeting. Had it really only been a week ago?

"And wouldn't you know it the credit card machine is working tonight."

Kenny laughed as she rung up the gas for his pump. He looked as if he were about to say something else, but the bell over the door sounded and caught both of their attentions. The group of guys who were with him all came into the store.

Good grief. Wasn't there some kind of law that said guys who looked this good couldn't travel together? She took in the good looks of each one of them. She appreciated their individual hotness on a female level but didn't feel anything close to what she felt when she looked at Kenny. Sure, they were all handsome, but just to look at Kenny had her struggling for breath.

"Hey, man, what's taking so long?" a tall blonde guy asked, walking up to the counter to stand beside Kenny.

He turned in her direction and flashed a huge grin. He had an infectious smile, and despite the fact she didn't have anything to smile about, she felt herself doing so.

"Well, who do we have here? What's your name, darling?" he asked, holding out his hand in greeting.

Her hand reached for his automatically.

"Connie," she answered.

She noticed a spark of recognition in his eyes as he shook her hand gently. Curious because she didn't think she had ever seen him before. She felt confident she would have remembered if she had.

"Hey, Joe, tone down the wattage on that thing will ya. You're liable to blind somebody," Kenny said, pointing towards his face. "And before the rest of you get any ideas about flashing your own pearly whites, she's taken."

Turning back to face her, Kenny gave her a wink, and her heart stopped beating.

"And we're just supposed to take your word for that, man? She might be ready to dump her lame ass boyfriend for a real man?" A tall, dark complexioned man pushed his way to the counter between Kenny and Joe.

"Hi, my name's Marcus. Nice to meet you," he said, reaching his hand out to her.

The smile he flashed her was a brilliant white across his dark skin. He was absolutely gorgeous. Connie didn't normally find men who shaved their heads attractive, but the one standing in front of her was the exception. He had the perfect shaped head for it, she found herself musing crazily. When she took his hand the warmth of his fingers wrapped around her own cold ones.

"Connie," she said softly, her gaze held by the glint of amusement in his onyx eyes.

"Hey, enough of that hand holding stuff," Kenny said, a frown creasing his brow, but she could see the smile in his eyes.

"I told you man she's taken already. So get your paws off."

"Yeah, but there are so many better looking men out there. Maybe she'd like to keep all her options open," another guy asked from the back.

He stood taller than the rest of his friends.

"Move it, Marcus," he said, pulling him out of the way and stepping to the counter. "Hi, beautiful, name's Troy."

Another perfect white smile was flashed in her direction. Connie had the crazy urge to pinch herself. She'd never had so many gorgeous men paying attention to her at one time before. She was definitely in the twilight zone.

"Hi," she said.

She glanced over at Kenny, uncertain as to what was going on.

"Will you guys get out of here? The store is only so big, and you guys are sucking up all the oxygen," he said, good naturedly elbowing Troy for his position at the counter.

"What you mean is you're scared she'll take one of us over you," a guy Connie hadn't yet met called from the back of the group.

She glanced in his direction. Her eyes widened at her first look at him. He had long black wavy hair that hung to his shoulders with sparkling blue eyes.

"Yeah, well, I don't think I have anything to worry about with that. Do I, Connie?" Kenny asked, a mischievous glint in his eyes.

Mesmerized by his look, she shook her head. No, he didn't have a thing to worry about with these guys. His friends were hot, but they didn't hold a candle to him.

"Alright, you guys," Kenny said, turning to his friends. "Get out."

Connie was surprised they complied with little grumbling and complaints. When it was once again just the two of them in the store, she breathed a sigh of relief. All that testosterone had been a bit overwhelming.

"Wow," she said under her breath.

"A little much, aren't they?"

He leaned a hip against the counter bringing him closer.

"Just a bit," she said, her stomach fluttering with nerves.

He had paid for his gas, so why wasn't he leaving with his friends. She glanced out the large store window and saw them either standing or sitting on their bikes in no apparent hurry.

"Your friends are waiting for you," she said softly.

Kenny glanced in the direction she'd been looking and hunched his shoulders.

"They're alright. Now that they've met you," he said, laughing.

Had she heard him right? They'd wanted to meet her?

"What? You told your friends about me?"

Why would he do that? They weren't together any longer.

"They wanted to know where I'd been all week because they hadn't heard from me. When I explained to them I had someone new in my life, they were anxious to meet you. Your being here tonight is strictly coincidence."

Connie was dumbstruck. She didn't know what to say.

"They're probably out there discussing your many assets," he said, his gaze raking over her ample breasts.

Her face got hot at his look, and she tried to ignore her body's reaction. It would have been easier if her body wasn't strumming with a desire that matched the heat in his gaze.

"Why would you tell them about me?"

"Isn't it obvious, Connie," he said, leaning across the counter.

He caressed her cheek with his palm and brushed his lips against her open mouth.

"I'll see you later."

In a daze, she watched him saunter across the parking lot back to his bike and his friends. As she watched him pumping his gas, she wondered if they were really talking about her. How had she stacked up? Had they liked her? Were they comparing her to the other women Kenny had introduced them to? Were they comparing her to Lori? A few moments later, they climbed on their bikes and revved up. They all turned in her direction and waved before they stormed off as quickly as they'd come.

Connie leaned against the counter a small smile on her face. Well, she'd been right. Kenny was out with someone as equally as gorgeous as he was. A giggle bubbled up and out of her throat.

Chapter 24

Sunday morning brought bright sunshine spilling into Connie's bedroom. She closed her eyes tight and pulled her pillow over her head. She thought she'd made sure to close her blinds when she'd gone to bed this morning. Reaching for the covers, she attempted to pull them up over her head but found them stuck on something. The more she tugged the more they resisted.

"Ugh," she said, throwing the pillow off her head.

"I had you pegged for a morning person. I guess I was wrong," a deep voice called from her room.

Connie sat up in bed, her eyes wildly searching. When her tired, gritty eyes landed on a fresh looking Kenny, she told her heart to settle down.

"You scared me," she yelled. "How did you get in?" she asked, falling back on the bed, her hands across her eyes.

She was in no mood to deal with him so early in the morning. Her body was still strumming from their encounter last night. She hadn't had enough time to build up any kind of resistance. Connie glanced at her clock on her nightstand through her fingers. It was barely eight. She'd gotten off from work at three but hadn't managed to fall asleep until about six because her mind had been full of thoughts of him. She had replayed his visit to the store several times over, trying to decipher its meaning each time. So she'd only been asleep for roughly two hours. Definitely not enough time to deal with the maleness of him.

"Your roommates let me in. I brought breakfast," he said, lifting a bag from beside the chair where he was lounging comfortably.

Connie peeked out from under her arm and saw the Krispy Crème donut bag. Oh, her weakness. In spite of her irritation over being awakened out of her much needed sleep, a part of her couldn't help but be touched that he remembered. She didn't doubt that inside the bag were glazed donuts. Why was he making this so difficult for her?

"What are you doing here, Kenny?"

He got up from the chair he'd been occupying in the corner of her room and moved to sit on the bed beside her. He pushed her over a little to make room for himself.

"Like I said, I brought you breakfast. I'll just put it on the nightstand and let you get back to sleep."

Soft fingers brushed her wayward hair back from her forehead. Her eyes closed against the tenderness of his touch. He needed to leave before she did something stupid. No, not stupid. Before she did what she longed to do.

"Kenny, please…" she pleaded.

He had to know what his touch was doing to her.

"Please what, Connie?"

He stroked her cheek before moving down the long length of her neck. She tilted her head to the side to allow him access. His thumb rubbed sensually against her pulse point in her neck. She was sure he could feel the erratic beat of her pulse and know how his touch was affecting her. It was waking her body up more effectively than anything else could have done. Connie felt the familiar tightening of her nipples as the material of her night shirt scratched the peaks. She shifted her legs as an ache began to throb between them to match the beat of her pulse.

"I need you," she whispered, staring up into his darkened gaze.

She slid her hand across his chest, feeling its hardness before pulling him down closer to her.

"I need you, too, Connie. But I need you for longer than a few hours. And until you can wrap your beautiful mind around that I won't settle for less."

Soft lips brushed hers. When she tried to deepen the kiss, he moved away and stood beside the bed staring down at her.

"Good luck on finals this week. I'll call you," he said, stroking her hair once more before leaving her room.

Connie blew out a frustrated breath. This was the oddest breakup she had ever been through. How was she ever supposed to get over him if every time she turned around he was there? Not to mention seeing him only served to remind her of what she was missing out on. Even after just a few minutes in his presence, she was wound so tight she wanted to scream in frustration. What was she going to do? Connie flipped over on her stomach, punching her pillow and prayed for the escape of sleep.

*****

Kenny stood outside Connie's door, his head down with his eyes closed. He didn't know where he'd found the will power to get up and leave. He'd seen the hardening of her nipples against her t-shirt, and it had caused an answering response in his own aroused body. His dick had stretched painfully against his zipper. As it was now, it was taking everything he had not to walk back into her room and put them both out of their misery.

Feeling someone watching him, he lifted his head to find Tracy standing in front of him. She was the last roommate he'd met. She stood there a concerned look clearly showing in her amber eyes, but the hint of a small smile played around the corners of her mouth.

"She kicked you out?"

"Nope, I left on my own," he replied, straightening.

"Are you gonna stick it out or are you gonna run south with your tail between your legs?"

The question caught him off guard and caused his temper to flare. It was on the tip of his tongue to ask her who the hell she was to ask him a question like that, but he held his tongue.

"I plan to stick it out," he said, pushing away from the wall and moving down the hall.

He needed as many people on his side as he could get, and Kenny didn't think it would help his cause to alienate one of Connie's roommates.

"Do you know why she ran?" Tracy called after him.

Kenny stopped in his tracks.

"I have a pretty good idea."

"She's had a pretty hard time with guys …. Well, with guys who look like you."

Kenny heard the hint of humor in her voice and again bit his tongue. Guys who looked like him. What the hell was that supposed to mean?

"I got the impression it was guys in general," he said, standing still his back towards her.

"Yeah, Connie hasn't done too well with ordinary guys either. But mostly it's you pretty boys who have done the most damage."

She moved to stand beside him.

"Come on, let's go downstairs and talk. Connie would be pissed if she found out I was meddling."

Kenny followed her downstairs and into the kitchen where they found Jamie and Tammy sitting at the kitchen table. He was still smarting a little over the pretty boy comment, but any information they could give him to help him understand where Connie's head was he would gladly take.

"Good morning, gorgeous," Tammy said, smiling at him.

"Back at ya," Kenny replied, returning her smile.

"You want a cup of coffee? You look like you could use one," Jamie said, turning from her position at the counter.

Kenny took a seat at the table and ran a hand down his face. Yeah, he guessed he had looked and definitely felt better.

"Yeah, that would be great. Thanks."

"So did Tracy tell you why we wanted to talk to you?" Jamie asked, taking a seat with them at the table.

He glanced at Tracy and shook his head.

"We've known Connie since we all met in middle school. We have sat and watched her get into all the wrong relationships for years. With the worse of it being in high school," Tammy began.

Groans came from the other two women at the table as they recalled those times.

"After a while we just stopped trying to tell her the guy was all wrong and let her find out for herself and would be here for her when it inevitably fell apart."

"Always when Connie found out, she swore it would never happen again. That she would never allow a guy to use her like that. Eventually, she just stopped dating anybody that looked halfway decent and then not at all," Jamie said.

"The first night you knocked on the door, I was like, "Oh, no, here we go again." I mean it had been almost a year since Connie had dated anyone, and then for her first one to be with you," Tammy gave a deep sigh that told of her frustration.

All he could do was laugh. It explained a lot about the first night he'd met her.

"I had wondered at the less than friendly greeting I received," he commented, a smile on his face.

"I'm sorry about that," she said, laughing.

"I guess I should apologize too then," Jamie said, a smile on her face. Her blue eyes twinkled with amusement. "When I came downstairs and saw you standing in the foyer asking for Connie, I thought we were about to cover the same ground again, and I wasn't having it. But when you looked at us but didn't look at us, I knew there was something different about you. Does that make sense?"

Laughter rumbled out of him as he looked over at Jamie. She really was cute.

"Complete sense," he said.

"I wasn't here that night, but when I got home and Tammy and Jamie were telling me about you, I must admit I was a little more skeptical then they were. Even after they told me how you had shut Brenda down, I was still reluctant to believe you could be different."

"And now?"

A smile titled her lips up.

"Now I believe you could be what our Connie needs in her life. She's been so happy this past week. Even Brenda and her negative ass hasn't been able to bring her down. Or so we thought," Tracy said, glancing at her friends.

"We just wanted you to know why Connie pushed you away. We didn't want you to think it's because she's a basket case or something," Tammy said.

"She's just somebody who hasn't had the best of luck with guys who ….," Tracy paused.

"Who look like me," he finished for her, nodding his head.

He glanced around the table at Connie's friends and wondered if she truly knew how lucky she was to have them. When he'd told his own friends about Connie, they had given him a hard time about her age, but they'd all been supportive and wanted to meet her. Then he'd had to explain she had dumped him. After their laughter had died down, they'd asked him what he was gonna do about it to which he'd responded without missing a beat that he was probably gonna marry her. Kenny could still recall the surprised looks on their faces. That was right before they began arguing about who would be best man.

"So you are gonna stick around, right?" Tammy asked, a frown between her arched eyebrows.

"Of course, he is," Tracy answered for him. "He loves her. Don't you?"

The answering smile on his face said more than words ever could. A myriad of emotions registered across Tammy and Jamie's faces before they each rushed from their chairs to embrace him. Kenny returned each of their hugs. Connie wasn't the only one who was lucky to have friends like these.

Chapter 25

Kenny dragged a tired body through his door on Thursday evening. He loosened his tie as he threw his briefcase on the counter. Without turning on any lights, he moved to the refrigerator and grabbed a beer. A sigh moved through his weary body as he tipped the ice cold bottle to his lips. He inhaled a deep breath and tried to let go of the past four days. He didn't think he'd worked longer hours in his life. He packed as much into a day as he could and didn't find himself leaving his office until sometimes eight or nine each night.

He headed upstairs, his beer in hand. He knew what he was doing, and it wasn't working. Dammit. He paused in his doorway. Another sigh moved through him before he walked into the room. Every time he looked at his bed, he saw Connie's curvaceous form in it. The sweet scent of jasmine still enticed him when he walked into his bathroom. When he closed his eyes too tired to keep them open any longer, it was dreams of Connie that came to him.

The way she laughed. The way she looked as he thrust into her heated center.

Sitting heavily on the side of his bed in his boxers, Kenny ran his fingers through his hair. He'd decided to let it grow out a little from his normal low cut. He loved the way Connie gripped his head when he was buried between her legs.

He shot up from the side of the bed. Dammit. He had to stop this. Every thought was filled with her. Waking or sleeping. He was going insane. The only thing that made his suffering better was the knowledge she was suffering as much as he was. Her roommates attested to the fact. He felt almost bad about his continued torture of her since she was in the middle of finals. They were both suffering, but only she had the power to put them out of their misery. He sure as hell hoped she opted to do it soon.

Kenny checked the time and reached for the phone. It was time for his nightly call. Since finals had begun, he'd opted to call instead of seeing her in person. Sunday had been enough for him to realize his will power wasn't up to where it needed to be just yet for face to face visits. It had taken everything in his power to walk out of her room. Coward, his brain taunted, and his fingers paused over the number pad of the phone. He didn't consider it being a coward. He considered it not pushing the limits of his control. But he had missed her, and he did want to see her. Kenny put the phone back on the base and moved towards his closet.

Twenty minutes later, he headed downstairs dressed in jeans and t-shirt. He set his alarm, grabbed his house keys from the counter where he'd left them and left his house on foot.

*****

Connie slammed her book closed and placed her elbows on top of it. If she didn't pull her mind back to the subject at hand, she'd fail her exam tomorrow. She pulled her gaze away from the clock over the stove. She'd come downstairs almost an hour ago to study at the kitchen table instead of her room but as of yet hadn't accomplished much. Her gaze kept straying to the digital numbers of the clock. She had watched the time tick pass seven-thirty. Anticipation had begun to build. When the numbers displayed eight o'clock, a smile had come to her face, and she'd looked down at the cordless phone that lay on the table beside her. Any minute now it would ring. That's what she'd been telling herself for the past thirty minutes.

Rising from the table, Connie put the phone back on its cradle. Incredible sadness washed over her. She felt tears threatening at the backs of her eyes. Kenny hadn't failed to call her every night this week at eight o'clock on the dot. Sometimes he'd still be in his office or on the way home. Last night he'd called from his cell, the loud sounds of a people in the background. Connie had asked him about his location, not wanting to believe he'd call her while on a date with another woman. When he'd informed her he was at a business dinner and had been thinking of her, the smile that had split her face and the joy that had moved through her were unimaginable. To think he'd been in the middle of something and had stopped to call her. So why hadn't he called tonight? What if something had happened to him? What if he had been in a car accident or worse? She didn't exactly know what worse could be, but the thought had her heart pounding uncontrollably and her hand reaching for the phone again. This time to call him. Her hand paused midair as the thought of his being with another woman rushed across her mind. Oh god. A different kind of panic gripped her. What if she called him and he was on a date? No. She refused to think like that. There was some other reason why he hadn't called her yet.

"But how can you be sure," Brenda's voice sounded in her head. *"You dumped him, remember? He's a single hot, red-blooded male with a healthy sex drive. He has needs, Constance."*

Her hand fell from the phone. Her fingernails dug into her skin as she squeezed her hand tight.

"No," Connie said aloud.

Kenny was different than any other guy she'd ever known before, and therefore he deserved a little more consideration than she'd given him. Even after she'd walked away from him, he'd remained in her life. A constant reminder of what he was offering her. If he wanted to date other people, then surely he would have said so. He wouldn't have made sure to call her every day. He wouldn't have introduced her to his friends.

Connie reached for the receiver once more, this time she managed to punch in his home number. Her heart pounded in her ears as she waited anxiously for him to pick up. When his voice mail clicked on, the debate began over whether or not to leave a message. What would she say? I went into a panic when you didn't call.

"Kenny, it's Connie. I just wanted to give you a call because ...," she hesitated before taking a deep breath. "I wanted to call because you were on my mind. Give me a call when you get a chance."

The doorbell chimed before she could scrutinize her message and its possible implications. She didn't want to ponder on it too much. Besides it was done now and she couldn't take the message back.

She was at the door when she hesitated. Maybe she should call one of her roommates down to answer it in case it was Brenda. She had been ducking her for the last few days and wasn't ready to face her yet. Brenda didn't know she and Kenny were no longer an item. She'd deliberately not told her because she hadn't wanted to hear any of what her sister might have to say on the matter. And she definitely didn't want to see the smug smile she was confident Brenda wouldn't even try to hide. Taking a deep breath when the bell chimed again, she opened the door. Kenny stood there smiling down at her. Relief hit her square in the face, and she pulled him inside and hugged him before she had a chance to think about it. He wasn't hurt, and what's more, he wasn't out with another woman. Strong arms returned her hug. Connie closed her eyes, enjoying the feel of his arms around her for just a moment longer before she moved away, embarrassed over her actions.

"I take it that means you're happy to see me," Kenny said, his eyes moving slowly over her body.

The immediate response to his perusal came as no surprise. She lowered her head before he could see the heat in her gaze.

"I called you a few minutes ago, but you didn't answer," she said instead of answering his question. "I was a little worried."

His fingers lifted her chin until her gaze met his. Heat smoldered in his eyes and her chest tightened.

"I left my cell phone at home. I'm sorry to have worried you, but I must say I'm glad for the reaction."

He held her gaze a few moments more before he released her chin and diverted his eyes to just over her shoulder. Connie saw the labored rise and fall of his chest and realized he was struggling with his emotions just as badly as she was.

"What are you doing here?"

Desperately she wanted him to say it was because he couldn't bear to stay away a moment longer. Then he'd take her in his arms and they'd head upstairs to make love. It had been six long, sexually frustrating days since she'd felt his wonderful weight upon her, thrusting into her deep core. A shiver danced up her spine. She had to get control of her thoughts or else they'd drive her crazy. Who was she kidding? She was already going insane. Her body was constantly on fire, and only one person could douse the flames. Even now the throbbing between her legs grew more intense the longer she stood close to him.

"It's been a rough week … at work, and I needed to get out for a while to get some air. You know clear my head and relieve some tension," he said, leaning against the door.

Connie was grateful for even the small amount of distance he'd put between them. But his eyes still roamed over her body with an intensity that licked the flames of her own desire. It took everything in her to stand there under the scrutiny.

"Have you lost weight?" he asked, tilting his head to the side.

It had a tendency to happen when you didn't eat. And she hadn't had an appetite since last week. At least one good thing was coming out of this whole fiasco.

"Yeah, a little I guess," she said, forcing her body to move.

Connie motioned for him to follow her into the kitchen.

"Why?"

Concern laced his simple question. It warmed her insides. Any other guy would have told her good but not Kenny.

"Not that it would hurt for me to drop a few pounds …," she began in a teasing voice.

"You don't need to drop a few of anything," he said, his voice coming out rough with irritation at her kidding on herself. "You look great just the way you are."

Kenny had always been good for her ego and self-esteem. Not once had he ever said a disparaging word about her need to lose weight or the way she dressed. Connie paused. Then, what was the problem again? Why had she gotten rid of this man?

"Thank you," she answered quietly still deep in her thoughts.

"I only speak the truth."

He picked up one of her text books from the table. "How did exams go today?"

Glad for the change in subject she filled him in on how her tests had gone that day and what she was currently trying to study. She wasn't surprised when he offered to help her. For the next two hours, they were immersed in a Q & A session.

"Wow, I hadn't realized it was so late," he said, getting up to stretch. "I'd better head home."

Connie glanced at the clock over the stove. It was a little after eleven. She hated to see him go, but he had to work tomorrow and she had more exams.

"Okay. Thanks for helping me study," she said, following him back out to the foyer.

"No problem. I just hope I actually helped you and not the opposite. It's been awhile since I was in college."

A frown puckered her brow.

"No one would be able to tell it by looking at you," she said, her gaze moving appreciatively over his handsome face.

A hint of color showed on his face and her smile widened.

"Thank you," he said softly.

"Just speaking the truth."

They stood staring at each other. Connie wasn't sure who moved first, but suddenly they were within a breath of each other. Her breathing came out labored, causing her breasts to rise and fall noticeably. He was so close all she had to do was just reach out to him.

"I had better get going," he said but didn't move.

"Kenny…."

She called his name on a sigh. Someone moved bringing them closer. The hardened outline of his erection pressed against her stomach. She wanted it inside of her. Before she could change her mind, Connie reached up and looped her hands around his neck.

"Connie, I don't think this is a good idea," Kenny said but didn't move away.

She pulled his head down until her lips were inches from their target. Her tongue stroked his parted lips. When he gasped, she claimed his mouth fully. Connie closed her eyes and sighed as pleasure moved through her. She thrust her tongue between his lips and made a sweep of his mouth. She felt and heard his groan of pleasure as he wrapped his arms around her waist, pulling her closer to the heat of his body. When she felt as if her lungs would collapse from lack of air, he lifted his head. His eyes were glazed over with desire. The same desire Connie was sure could be seen in her own eyes.

"Kenny, I want you," she whispered against his neck.

She placed hot kisses against his skin. Strong hands moved from her waist down over the curve of her ass to pull her closer against his hardened member.

"I want you, too, Connie. But I don't want you on a temporary basis. I want you in the forever way."

He moved his hips to thrust against her center before he reached behind his neck to remove her hands. Kenny brought her fingers to his lips and kissed them softly.

"When you're ready for that, let me know. I only hope it's before we both die of sexual frustration."

With that he was gone.

Connie stood there in the foyer, her arms hanging loose by her side. She felt emptier than she'd felt in days. Her body ached in places only Kenny knew how to touch.

"Oh, Constance, you need to rethink some things," she told herself as she headed back towards the kitchen.

Chapter 26

At four o'clock Friday afternoon, Connie breathed her first real breath all week. It was over. She had just taken her final test of the school year. Whew! She thought she'd done pretty well, but she would have to wait a few weeks to find out exactly how well. It was now eight o'clock, and she was on her way to the gas station. Roger had called to see if she could come in early to cover for someone who'd called out sick. Since she didn't have anything else planned, she'd automatically said yes. When she walked into the store, he greeted her with a smile of relief.

"Constance, thanks so much for coming in. My wife and I have made plans for the evening, and she would kill me if I had to cancel on her," Roger said, heading towards the backroom.

"It's no problem. Not like I have a life," she said under her breath.

"What's that, hon?" he asked, coming back out.

"Nothing. I didn't have anything planned tonight anyway."

"Okay, but I owe you. Why don't you take tomorrow night off? You just finished up finals, right?"

Connie nodded.

"Well, it's settled. I'll work for you tomorrow night, and you go out and have a good time. Release some steam. I remember how it was during finals. But anyways thanks again," he said and headed out the door.

*****

It had been a slow night for Connie. With classes over, there was nothing to occupy her thoughts. An image of Kenny and how he'd looked standing in the foyer last night before he had left sprang to mind. Just the thought of him …. The bell chiming over the door signaling someone had entered cut off where her errant thoughts had been heading. Automatically her gaze moved to the clock on the wall. Almost one o'clock. She looked up to see an attractive African American woman walking towards the counter. Connie felt her own lips lift in response to the warm smile the woman was giving her. A strange sense of familiarity washed over her. No name came readily to mind. Maybe she had been in the store another night she had worked.

"Hi," Connie said in greeting.

She tilted her head and studied the woman now standing directly in front of her. She couldn't shake the feeling that she knew her. Connie wracked her brain trying to figure out where she'd seen her before.

"Hello," the woman said, staring at her in return.

"Can I help you with something?"

"No, I just wanted to come by to get a look at you. You're very pretty," the woman replied, a sparkle in her brown gaze.

A frown creased Connie's brow.

"I beg your pardon. Do I know you?"

"No, but I believe you and I will be great friends. That is as long as you don't tell my son I disobeyed him by coming here," she said, laughing out loud. "My name is Marcelle. Marcelle Jamison."

No wonder this woman looked familiar to her. She was Kenny's mother. Connie shook the offered hand in greeting wondering why she was here. She had said it was to get a look at her. Embarrassment moved through her as she glanced down at what she had on. Another of her famous baggy sweats and oversized t-shirt ensembles. A sigh filled her lungs. Oh, well, it didn't make any difference.

"My son has finally gotten it right I'm happy to say. So why is it you and he are not engaged yet?" Marcelle asked, her face openly curious.

Connie's mouth opened in surprise but no words came out. Engaged? What should she say? She didn't think it her place to break the news to Kenny's mother that they were no longer together, but what choice did she have?

"I'm sorry, Mrs. Jamison," she began.

"Please call me Marcelle. Mrs. Jamison was my husband's mother," she said with a wave of her hand. "May she rest in peace."

"Mrs. Jamison, Kenny and I aren't seeing each other any longer," she said instead.

She didn't think she had the right to address her by her first name given the circumstances.

"Yes, that's what he told me, but I'm curious about whose decision that was."

It sounded as if she already knew the answer. Yet Connie found herself hesitating under Marcelle's close scrutiny.

"Mine," she said quietly, not meeting her gaze.

"And why would you do that, dear? My son is quite a catch or so I've heard," Marcelle said, smiling.

Pride for her eldest son shined brightly on her face. And she should be proud of him. Even though they were no longer together, Connie could not deny the fact that Kenny was a wonderful man. He would make some woman very happy. He had made us very happy while he was here, her heart reminded her. And if you give him the chance, I bet he would be willing to do it again.

"Yes, he is," Connie admitted.

"Then, I'm confused? I know he cares for you deeply. I see it in his eyes when he speaks of you."

Her eyes widened in shock. First, his friends and now his mother. All of this after she had kicked him out of her life.

"He's spoken to you of me? Recently?"

Marcelle leaned against the counter, her smile never wavering.

"Yes, he has. My son is quite taken with you. Why don't you put him out of his misery and I dare say yourself as well, and go to him?"

It sounded so easy when someone else said it. But Connie knew otherwise.

"It's not as simple as it might seem. I have a problem putting my trust in the right man," Connie said before snapping her mouth closed.

Embarrassed by her comment, she lowered her gaze. What had she been thinking to confide in Kenny's mother of all people? But the look of compassion and concern that had been in her gaze had drawn the truth from her before she'd been able to stop it.

"And Kenny's done something to cause you to doubt him? He's proven he can't be trusted with your heart?" His mother prodded softly.

Connie shook her head slowly, answering no to all of the above.

"You know, dear, it's not fair to condemn him for the actions of others. When Kenny's father and I met, it just so happened to be days after an incident on our college campus. A few white boys had taken it upon themselves to pick on a few of us black girls. Now if I had held that against James, I would have missed out on the best years of my life. Not to mention, I would have deprived you of ever meeting my son. All because I took my anger out on him because he looked like those who had harassed us. As it turned out, James' looks were one of the perks to dating him. He's quite a handsome devil even to this day."

Love sparkled in Marcelle's eyes at the thought of her husband. That's the kind of love she wanted to have with someone. No matter how much time passed, it never faded. Someone she could …. Trust with her heart.

"It's not that simple for me," Connie began, shaking her head. "Kenny's so … and well, I'm just … not. How can someone like him ever be truly happy with someone like me? I am so far removed from what he's used to. I mean he's gorgeous, and I'm … cute."

Frustration over the situation got the best of her suddenly. It wasn't fair for her to finally meet a man who seemed to like her as she was and he turned out to look like all the other men who had ever hurt her. Talk about irony.

"Dear, surely you aren't saying you broke up with my son because he's too handsome," Marcelle asked, amusement in her voice. "Why I don't believe I've ever heard that one before."

At the look of amusement on her face, Connie lowered her head to her hands. Great, now Kenny's mother thought she was some kind of fruitcake.

"Connie," Marcelle's warm, soothing voice called.

Embarrassment kept her head lowered until she felt a warm touch on her hair.

"Constance."

Connie raised her head to see the look of amusement gone. In its place was an understanding that could only come from one who knew. Marcelle reached across the counter to take Connie's hand in her warm grasp.

"You know love comes in all kinds of unexpected packages. It's up to you to decide if you want to simply sit and admire the way the package is wrapped. Taking in the tight corners, all the beautiful colors and the pretty bow on top. Or if you want to take the chance that what's inside is ten times better than the way it's wrapped. It's never easy to give it just one more try when we've been hurt before. But when you meet that someone who takes up your every waking moment with thoughts of them …."

Marcelle's eyes were closed and the sweetest of smiles graced her face. When her eyes opened, they shimmered brightly.

"Let's just say you owe it to yourself to give it a chance because you deserve it."

Marcelle gave Connie's hand a gentle squeeze and left the store. For a long time, Connie stood rooted to the same spot. Her thoughts filled with what Marcelle had said and then of her time spent with Kenny. From the beginning, he had filled up not just her waking thoughts but her sleeping ones as well, starring in her dreams from their first meeting. And when they were together, everything seemed to be better. He never let her put herself down and had seemed to make it his personal mission to begin filling in the gaps where her self-esteem was lacking. He paid attention to her and seemed to be able to see everything there was to her even when she said nothing. Even since they had broken up, he had still remained a constant in her life. Calling her to check on finals. Helping her study. Telling her she didn't need to lose a pound because there was nothing wrong with the way she looked. No, not much had seemed to change this week with the exception they weren't having sex. Connie could admit that while her body craved his, it wasn't all she'd missed about him. She missed that special smile that was just for her. The look in his eyes when he saw her. The way she felt when she was wrapped in his arms.

All her life she'd dreamed of having the guy that all the women looked at with longing. She'd wanted to be the one with the guy on her arm who made heads turn. Male and female. But in addition to that, she had wanted a man who made her feel beautiful. Connie had wanted to have a man who when he looked at her, he saw the real her.

"Oh my God," she said aloud.

She'd had it all within her grasp, but she'd thrown it away because …. Well, because he had looked too damned good to be true, and she couldn't imagine he would truly want her. But Kenny did. It was in the way he'd held her the first night they'd made love. It was in his eyes last night before he'd left.

Glancing at her watch, Connie promised herself she would make it right as soon as she could. She was ready to go after what she wanted. She wanted to open the box with the pretty wrapping paper because inside she knew what she'd find.

Chapter 27

Connie awoke with a start and sat straight up in bed. Her eyes darted around her darkened bedroom searching for her clock.

"Oh, no," she whispered, her voice raspy with sleep.

It was after eight o'clock Saturday night. What had happened?

When she had gotten off this morning, she had headed over to Kenny's house. She had wanted to tell him what she had discovered in the wee hours of this morning and hadn't wanted to wait. She had stood ringing the bell for a good five minutes, but he hadn't been home. The key she still had to his house had almost burned a hole in her pocket, but she had refrained from using it. Reluctantly, she had headed home. On the way she had called and left him a message on his home phone and tried his cell, reaching voice mail there as well. Connie had forced herself to stay up, not wanting to miss his call, but her body had been weary and shaking from lack of sleep. Finally at about ten o'clock, she'd had to admit to herself she needed some rest. Her eyes had burned from being forced to remain open. She'd promised herself she would only sleep for a little while, and then she'd try him again. A little while had turned into all afternoon and most of the evening if her clock could be believed. Though she hated to admit it, she did feel refreshed. Sleep had not come easy this week with finals and then the whole thing with Kenny.

Swinging her legs over the side of her bed, she reached for the phone. She quickly scrolled through the calls and felt a moment of disappointment when she saw no evidence of his returning any of her calls. Not allowing any doubts to set in, she dialed his home number again. As she listened to the ringing on the other end, dread pooled in the pit of her stomach. Where was he? Why hadn't he called her back? She'd left him four messages between home and his cell phone. She tried to remain positive, but it was hard when doubts were threatening to beat her down.

"No," she told herself firmly. "He is not with another woman. There is some other reason to why he hasn't returned my call yet."

She recalled the last time she hadn't been able to reach him, and worry and dread had begun to set in. He had just shown up on her doorstep. It had been as if he had known she wanted and needed to see him. When the doorbell chimed, Connie dropped the phone on the bed and practically flew down the steps.

"I got it," she called to her friends, her hand on the doorknob.

The look of expectancy died on her face when she opened the door to find Brenda standing there. Connie tried not to allow the disappointment to show on her face too badly but knew she'd failed at Brenda's greeting.

"Wishing for him to show up or call didn't work when you were younger, Constance, and it won't work now," Brenda said, moving pass her to enter the foyer.

Connie made a face at her back and closed the door. Brenda gave her a once over and shook her head.

"When will you ever learn to stay within your realm of men and leave the others to those of us who can handle them? Look at yourself. Don't you ever get tired of being the butt of the joke?"

The smug look in Brenda's gaze was meant to put Connie back in her place. In the past it may have worked, but tonight as she stood staring back at her sister, all it did was piss her off.

"You know when I was younger I used to go to bed each night and pray I could be more like you," she began.

"That's understandable," Brenda said, a smile on her face.

Connie smiled sweetly in return.

"As I got older, I used to beg God to allow me to wake up the next morning as an only child."

The look of surprise on her sister's face brought a small smile to hers.

"Why are you here?" she asked, her hands on her hips.

"I came by to see if your little romance had dissolved into thin air yet," she said, giving Connie the once over again. "And I guess I have my answer, don't I."

Connie simply smiled at Brenda before turning to head back upstairs before stopping with her hand on the rail. For years she had endured her sister's negative words and attitude without saying anything in her defense. On any other day, she would have merely headed to her room to hide her pain behind closed doors but not today. She turned back to her sister and gave her the once over. For the first time allowing herself to see Brenda not as the ex-model but as the person she really was. A horrible individual who had made it her life's goal to make her younger sister's life miserable.

"You know, Brenda, I'm not sure what it is that I ever did to you to make you dislike me so much. I don't know whether it's because I'm younger than you and when I came along you were no longer the center of attention. But whatever the reason, you need to get over it. And until you do, I don't need or want you in my life. I love you because you are my sister and our parents raised me to love family, but that is where it ends."

Connie walked over to the door and opened it.

"Goodbye, Brenda."

For long moments, she didn't know if her sister was going to leave or not, but she was determined to stand there as long as it took for her to walk through that door. Brenda paused when she got to her, and for half a moment Connie thought she was going to say something, but she didn't. She simply walked quietly through the door, and Connie closed it just as quietly behind her. She leaned against the door her head down. Unexpectedly, tears burned the backs of her eyes. Feeling eyes on her, she looked up to see her roommates coming down the stairs towards her.

"You ok, Con?" Jamie asked.

The shock on the faces of her roommates was almost laughable. It was rare she said a disparaging word about Brenda, let alone to her face. But tonight had been the right time. She nodded her head and moved away from the door and headed upstairs, a little in shock over what had happened.

Walking into her room, Connie closed her door and lay back down on her bed. It wasn't long before she found herself back up pacing beside it. Restlessness was setting in. Now that she had made a decision to have Kenny in her life, she was ready to take action. She glanced at the phone and wondered if she should call him again. Her hand hesitated, hovering above it. She'd already called and left several messages that hadn't been returned. What was one more call going to accomplish? She pulled her hand away and turned her back on the phone. Dammit. She was doing it again. Allowing her insecurities to get the better of her.

With determination blazing in her eyes, she grabbed the phone and punched in Kenny's cell phone number.

Ring ... ring...

"Hello?"

Connie hesitated. That wasn't Kenny.

"I'm sorry I must have dialed the wrong number," she said, preparing to hang up.

"No, wait, are you looking for Kenny?"

"Yes."

"Hang on a second. Can I say who's calling?" the male voice questioned.

"Connie."

She tried not to put any thought into why he was asking who she was. Or why someone else was answering Kenny's cell phone.

"Oh, hey. It's Troy. Hang on a minute, honey."

Connie heard him yell for Kenny.

"Hey, sweetheart, what's up."

Kenny's deep voice came across the lines washing over her. She plopped down on the edge of the bed before her legs gave out on her. Suddenly the pressure she'd been under over the last week got the better of her, and she began to cry.

"Connie."

She heard Kenny call her name, but she couldn't pull herself together enough to answer him to save her life. Her mouth moved, and she heard sounds coming out but nothing legible.

"Connie, are you alright?"

The voices of his friends questioning if everything was alright could be heard in the background. Their concern for her, a stranger, someone they had only met once caused the tears to flow harder.

"I'm on my way. I'll be there in ten minutes," he said and disconnected the call.

The phone fell from her numb fingers as she ran her fingers through her hair. All the years of pain she'd endured at the hands of others poured out of her. She cried for the love she'd almost lost and for the love she'd found with Kenny. Connie curled up on her bed, her arms wrapped tightly around herself. Kenny was on his way. He'd make it all better.

Chapter 28

Kenny pulled his bike up to the curb outside of Connie's house. He glanced around at his friends, who'd all insisted on coming with him. They hadn't gotten to know Connie but had all agreed if she was important to him, then she was important to them. Not bothering with taking off his helmet, he swung his leg over the back of his bike and strode towards the door. He heard his friends all dismounting behind him and eventually brought up the rear.

He rang the doorbell and pulled his helmet off his head. A smiling Jamie answered the door.

"Hey, Kenny, what are you doing here?"

"Connie called me crying. Is she here?" he asked, walking into the foyer.

The look of confusion on her face threatened to tax his patience further.

"Crying. Yeah, she's upstairs I think," she said.

That was all he needed to know. He bound up the steps taking them two at a time. When he reached Connie's door, he didn't bother to knock, he just burst in. The sight of her balled up on her side, her body shaking from her low sobs ripped at his heart.

"Connie," he said softly, kneeling beside the bed.

He placed his hand on her shoulder. She rolled over and his heart stopped beating. Her eyes were puffy from crying. Her nose was running.

"Oh, sweetheart. Don't cry. Please don't cry," he said, wrapping his arms around her.

He heard voices behind him in the doorway, but none of that mattered as he continued to hold her. He was briefly aware of the door closing to offer them some privacy.

When her body stopped shaking, Kenny lifted his head from where it had been buried in her neck. He pushed the hair away from her tear stained cheeks.

"What happened? Was it Brenda?"

Kenny swore if it was she was done.

"It was everything," Connie said, her voice raspy from her tears. "It was the stress of this week. Last week and all the weeks before that."

Guilt rode him hard. He knew he hadn't made things easy for her after she'd told him to leave. To think he had been a part of her breakdown. He hadn't wanted to make things worse, but it appeared his being in her life had caused her pain.

"I'm sorry, Connie. I should have listened to you when you told me to leave. I never meant to hurt you," he said, lowering his gaze, not wanting to see the accusation in her eyes.

A soft hand stroked the side of his face.

"Kenny."

He couldn't bring himself to look at her. He was afraid of what he'd see.

"Kenny, look at me," came the soft request.

Against his will, his chin lifted until he was looking into shimmering eyes. The soft smile on Connie's face confused him.

"The only pain you caused me was of a physical kind. The way my body has ached for yours this week should be a crime. Other than that, you have done nothing but try to show me what I could have if I'd stop being too scared to believe."

She sat up on the bed causing him to move back a little. She placed both hands on his face and pulled him towards her and bestowed upon him one of the sweetest kisses he had ever known. The tenderness of her touch caused his heart to ache. When he pulled back, the look shining in the depths of her eyes was blinding. Dare he believe she was finally ready to accept what he was offering?

"I have missed you more than I ever thought it possible to miss someone. And I realized everything I had been looking for was right in front of me. Who needs a fantasy man when I can have you in living breathing reality?"

"Connie, I need to hear you say it."

He held his breath while he waited for her to utter the words that would end his week of torment and allow the rest of his life to begin. The brilliance of the smile she graced him with threatened to blind him. She had no idea how truly beautiful she was. If he did nothing else, he swore to himself he would spend the rest of his life making her see what he saw when he looked at her.

"Kenny, I want the fantasy. I want to give us a chance. I want to see if reality can truly be better than my wildest dreams."

Kenny couldn't believe the weight that lifted from his shoulders at her words. He glanced at her to make sure she had on shoes then stood and reached for her hand. He pulled her behind him down the stairs. At the bottom, he paused.

"Should we tell them we're leaving?"

She moved suggestively against him.

"They'll figure it out on their own."

A shiver ran down Kenny's spine. He threw her a hot look full of promise of what was to come before heading out the door. Connie paused when she saw his bike sitting at the curb.

"I was out with the guys when you called me. I didn't have time to go home first," he said in way of explanation.

He realized he didn't have his extra helmet with him as he hadn't expected to have a rider. Kenny headed towards Troy's bike and retrieved the extra helmet he had.

"No, it's okay," she said, allowing herself to be strapped into the helmet.

Kenny got on first and offered her a hand as she straddled the bike behind him. the first time she'd ridden with him, she'd been cautious in her grip on him until they'd began moving and she'd realized she needed to hold on tight. This time her grip on him tightened as she pressed herself close to his back and he hadn't even started the damn bike. Kenny sent up a silent prayer that he'd be able to make it home safely. His dick was threatening to burst free of its confinement behind the zipper of his jeans.

"Hang on," he called over his shoulder as he turned his bike on.

He revved the engine and felt her grip around his waist tighten further. He didn't know if it was in nervousness or excitement. He hoped the latter was true. Pulling away from the curb, the front door opened and several pairs of eyes watched as they peeled off down the street.

Chapter 29

Connie opened her eyes to find herself outside
Kenny's home. She breathed deep the scent of the man she
loved. Her arms tightened around him. She didn't want to
ever let go.

"We're here," Kenny said, his gloved hands on top
of hers.

Reluctantly, her grip around his waist loosened. She
took the helmet off her head and shook her hair out.
Glancing to her left, she noticed he had already dismounted
from the bike and was holding his hand out to help her.
Connie smiled up at him and placed her hand trustingly in
his leathered grip.

They walked up the walkway holding hands as if
their lives weren't forever changed from this moment
forward. Nerves assaulted her as she walked ahead of him
into his home. Looking around now at his large foyer and
the steps that led to his bedroom, she realized this was
where she wanted to be. The door had barely closed before

she found herself pulled tight against Kenny's hard frame. She could feel his hardened length at the center of her own heat.

"I want you more than I can begin to tell you," he said against her lips.

Connie opened to allow him all the access he wanted. She felt his tongue sweep in and caress her bottom lip. She moaned her pleasure against his mouth before reaching her hands around to his backside and pulling him closer to her.

"Then how about you show me how much you want me. I can already feel it," she said, moving her throbbing clit against him.

Moisture pooled between her legs, and her knees threatened to buckle. Reaching up she pushed his leather jacket over his shoulders.

"Have I told you how hot you look in leather," she asked, working on the buttons of his shirt.

It soon joined his jacket on the foyer floor.

"No, you haven't." Kenny said, his breathing coming out in short gasps.

Connie placed kisses across the expanse of his muscled chest before tugging a hardened nipple into her mouth.

"Well, you do," she said, reaching for his hands, which were still encased in his leather gloves.

She stroked her cheek with his hands and her eyes closed as the soft buttery feel of the leather moved against her skin. She moved his hand down until it rested on her breast and squeezed causing him to palm her breasts. It seemed to be all the encouragement he needed. He made short work of her t-shirt, throwing it to the floor somewhere behind her and cupped her breasts again. Her nipples strained against the material of the bra she wore. Kenny pinched and pulled on them until they were swollen nubs and a familiar ache throbbed between her legs. Connie moved against the hardening dick pressed against her center. She needed and wanted more.

"Kenny, please," she begged, moving her head so his lips skimmed down her neck to her shoulder.

The warm feel of the leather moving across her skin was driving her slowly insane.

"Honey, I don't think we're gonna make it to the bedroom," he said against her ear.

"I don't need a bed. All I need is your dick in me and soon."

A groan sounded next to her ear before he grabbed her hand and dragged her behind him into the family room where he pushed her down on the couch. He paused only long enough to remove his gloves before joining her. He brushed a soft kiss against her open mouth and then moved down to her heaving chest. Taking an extended nipple in his mouth, he sucked it through her bra. Connie sighed in pleasure, placing her hand to the back of his head to hold him in place. Too soon he released her nipple, kissing his way down the swell of her stomach. He leaned up to help her take off her pants. The scrap of material, now soaked with her juices, seemed to hold his attention.

"You have more of these," he asked, fingering the material, brushing against her swollen clit as he did so.

Her breath came out in puffs as she tried to answer him as he continued stroking her aching clit.

"Yeah, at home."

"Good," he said, moving between her spread legs and pushing them farther apart to accommodate his large frame. "I like these a lot."

"Why?"

Kenny pulled the scrape of material up until it was pressed directly against her clit. He moved the material back and forth, causing friction.

"Oh, god," Connie screamed as pleasure shot through her body in waves.

"That's why." he said, lowering his head between her legs.

At the first touch of his tongue on her clit, a fresh wave of hot cum leaked from her pussy. Her head thrashed back and forth on the couch's pillow as he began to suck on her tight little nub. He flicked it with his tongue before moving lower to lap up the juices running freely from her opening. Pushing her panties to the side he moved two fingers against her.

"Oh, you are so wet."

Two fingers went inside, and her ass lifted up off the couch. She felt so full for the first time in days, and oh, it felt so good. Her mouth opened to scream, but no sound came out as he began moving his fingers in and out faster, her juices making it easy for him. His thumb began to stroke against her clit, and she had little time to prepare herself as her orgasm came hard and fast. This time when she opened her mouth to scream, she feared the whole neighborhood heard her.

"Oh, god, Kenny, I want your dick inside me now," she said, still riding his fingers.

Slowly, he pulled his drenched fingers out of her opening and licked them. Another rush of moisture slipped from her pussy as she watched him.

"Kenny, please I want your dick inside me," she begged while squirming beneath him.

In record time, he removed the rest of his clothes and was back on top of her before she could miss him. He pushed her legs further apart and inserted the tip of his dick into her wet center. Connie begged him for more. Putting the majority of his weight on his arms, he leaned up and pushed further into her moist heat. She tightened her cunt muscles around his dick pulling him further. As she began to move up and down along his length, he thrust harder, burying his straining dick deep into her pussy. She wrapped her long legs around his waist and pulled him tighter against her. She saw the straining muscles in his arms and the concentration he was using to remain in control. But she wanted him out of control. She wanted him to cum with her, and she was on the edge again. Connie used her cunt muscles to milk his dick along its length, and it felt so good.

"Oh, Connie, honey you have to stop doing that if I'm gonna last," he said, his breath coming out strained as he moved faster and harder into her.

"I want you to cum with me, and I'm so close," she said as she moved her fingers between their bodies and began to rub her clit.

Kenny watched as her fingers spread her lips and one finger swiped against the hardened little nub.

"Oh, I'm gonna cum," he said as he moved against her, moisture leaking from her hole each time he pulled out.

"Oh, yes, Kenny ... yes," she screamed.

Her cunt muscles tightened around his dick like a vice, and he couldn't hold off his orgasm any longer. Kenny gave a final thrust, forcing a fresh rush of liquid from her pussy and followed her over the edge.

*****

Kenny looked down at the woman wrapped in his arms and knew now was as perfect a time as any to tell her how he felt. He'd thought he'd need soft music, candle light. But all he'd really needed was her in his arms. In no time she had come into his life and turned it and him upside down. She had forced him to question what it was he was looking for in a woman, and all too soon he realized he didn't have a clue. He knew what society said he should look for. He knew what his friends had suggested he look for. But until he'd met Connie, he'd never truly been sure.

"I love you, Constance Banks," he said softly against her ear.

Kenny saw one eye open to look at him.

"Oh, yeah, and when did you decide that," she asked, opening her other eye to stare up at him.

"I think it all started when you stood behind the counter frowning at me. I found that kind of a turn on," he said, laughing down at her.

Connie smiled in return.

"Yeah, I'll bet. That's because it probably had never happened before."

"You're right, and I knew then and there that anyone who could resist my charm and still make me hot for them was a keeper."

"Yeah?" she asked, pulling him down and spreading her legs so he could feel how hot she was.

"Yeah. I think we need to take this to the bedroom," he said, getting off of her and reaching down to help her rise to her feet.

They walked hand in hand naked through the house, which was still dark since they hadn't bothered to turn on any lights when they'd come in. Reaching the bed, they both fell on top of the covers, arms and lips locked.

"Kenny," Connie said, looking up at him, her eyes soft.

He raised his head from where he'd been suckling her nipples.

"Hmm," he said, gently biting the peaks and pulling them until she sucked in her breath.

His hardened dick nudged against her moist opening seeking entry.

"I just wanted to say..." she began but stopped when he entered her in one stroke, taking the breath from her.

"Oh," she gasped.

Kenny leaned over her, moving his hips to slowly thrust into her pussy.

"You had something you wanted to tell me," he asked, looking down at the pleasure rolling across her face at his movements.

"I wanted to tell you...."

Kenny pulled out until just the tip of his dick was inserted inside.

"Yeah, sweetheart," he asked, strain showing on his face as he tried to hold onto his orgasm.

"I wanted to say I love you too," she ended on a high pitched scream as he slammed into her until his tip hit the back of her pussy, causing them both to gasp as their orgasm rolled over them.

Later they lay locked in each other's arms, each content in the fact they'd finally found what they had been looking for. Both had learned true beauty comes from the inside out instead of the opposite way. And that love can definitely be found in the most unexpected packages. Whether it was an oversized t-shirt and baggy sweat pants or an Armani suit.

The End

CPSIA information can be obtained at www.ICGtesting.com
Printed in the USA
245261LV00007B/69/P

9 780983 259534